Traditional

VEGETARIAN
COOKING

Traditional
VEGETARIAN
COOKING

Recipes from Europe's Famous
CRANK'S RESTAURANT

David & Kay Canter · Daphne Swann

Illustrations by John Lawrence

Healing Arts Press
Rochester, Vermont

Healing Arts Press
One Park Street
Rochester, Vermont 05767

LIBRARY OF CONGRESS CATALOGING-IN-PUBLICATION DATA

Canter, David.
   [Cranks recipe book]
   Traditional vegetarian cooking : recipes from
Europe's famous Cranks restaurants / David Canter,
Kay Canter, Daphne Swann; illustrated by John
Lawrence.
       p. cm.
     Reprint. Originally published: Cranks recipe book.
New York : Thorsons Publishers, 1985, c1982.
     Includes index.
     ISBN 0-89281-425-X
     1. Vegetarian cookery. I. Canter, Kay. II. Swann,
Daphne. III. Title.
   TX837.C34 1991
   641.5'636—dc20   91-11528
                                     CIP

Printed and bound in the United States.

10 9 8 7 6 5 4 3

Cover illustration by Elayne Sears
Cover design by Leslie Phillips

Healing Arts Press is a division of Inner Traditions International,
Ltd.

Distributed to the book trade in the United States by American
International Distribution Corporation (AIDC)

Distributed to the book trade in Canada by Book Center, Inc.,
Montreal, Quebec

Distributed to the health food trade in Canada by Alive Books,
Toronto and Vancouver

Contents

TO DAVID

Who was the founder, inspiration, and creative architect of Cranks.

David Canter died very suddenly on 1 July 1981. He dedicated many hours of work to the writing, production, and design of this book, which was almost completed at his death. We have tried to keep the book as close as possible to the original text and offer it as a tribute to his memory.

Acknowledgments

Cranks would not have succeeded or possessed its special character without the contributions of many staff, suppliers, and friends. We would like to thank them all, not only for their work on our behalf but for the little bit of themselves that has become part of the Cranks personality. In particular we would like to thank the following by name:

DAVID'S FATHER, Norman Canter, who lent us £500 for the first Cranks restaurant, and never asked for it back!

EDWARD BAWDEN, whose distinctive drawings ornamented our first brochure and are still used today.

DONALD JACKSON, whose calligraphy and graphics have contributed so much to the unmistakable style of Cranks.

JOHN LAWRENCE, the artist and illustrator, whose beautiful wood engravings adorn our literature.

RAY FINCH (and his team at Winchcombe), whose beautiful stoneware pottery has contributed so much to Cranks image and who has consistently and relentlessly supplied us with literally thousands of cups, saucers, bowls, plates, and so on over the years.

DAVID RANSOM, interior designer, who worked with David Canter on the design of Cranks restaurants and the Dartington Cider Press Centre.

JAMES AND SUE MORE-MOLYNEUX, of Loseley Park Farm, who started making yogurt in 1969 and, together with their son Mike, make our dairy products to such a high standard.

SAM MAYALL, of Pimhill in Shropshire, whose farm is a paragon of organic farming.

MIRIAM POLUNIN, who with sensitive expertise assisted us in restructuring some of the text.

JANE SUTHERING, for her invaluable work on the recipes and text.

SHIRLEY-ANNE DOWTHWAITE, our wonderful secretary, who has helped us in a thousand ways, in addition to the endless checking and typing of this book.

Our thanks to the countless others over the years who have worked for us; and, not least, our thanks to our current team and management.

Preface by David Canter

Traditional Vegetarian Cooking is our response to the thousands of our customers who have consistently asked us for the "know-how" of Cranks food. And now here are over 300 recipes which we are confident will bring the spirit of Cranks to you.

Kay Canter's own whole food recipes from home began the treasury in the early days. Twenty-two years later it has been enriched by the passing touches of many caring Cranks cooks, finding recipes, testing recipes, and making them work to perfection. Now this wide repertoire has been returned to the home scale. We know you will find they work, thanks to the efforts of Kay and the skills of delightful home economist Jane Suthering. Together they test-cooked in weekly sessions over eighteen months to satisfy our standards of taste and clear presentation. Some say we are crazy to give away our secrets to possible competitors! We hope you will enjoy trying them out in your own home.

The story of Cranks by David Canter

On our first day of business, 21 June 1961, we had no idea how much food to prepare. We had not advertised the opening of Cranks restaurant at 22 Carnaby Street, then a quiet backwater. So we were pleasantly surprised when a steady stream of people came in to fill our fifty seats. They saw a modest-sized ground floor and basement where every item of food and furnishing expressed the same values: simple natural materials used in a direct and craftsmanly way.

On the menu were mainly salads, of a completely different kind from what most of those new customers would have connected with the word. In contrast to the traditional tired lettuce that makes the appetite wilt too, these salads could change the eater's whole view of vegetables. The vivid combinations of ingredients and colors, crisp from fresh cutting and dressing, were teamed with equally fresh whole grain rolls, soups, savouries, and puddings. The quality of the materials used to make all these—only 100% whole grain flour, raw sugar, free-range eggs, fresh fruit, and dairy produce—was matched by the surroundings. Now familiar but then revolutionary to most people's eyes was the use of handthrown stoneware pottery, solid natural-colored oak tables, heather brown quarry tiles, woven basket lampshades and hand-woven seat covers, among the white painted brick arches of the bakeshop we had toiled to convert with a borrowed £500.

Both food and surroundings have changed only in detail during all the expansion of the next twenty-one years. They already expressed the ideals of Cranks three owners and partners, who, with our first helper Netty, formed the entire staff that busy day.

As the restaurant flourished in spite of being tucked away, we were delighted that so many other people wanted to seek out the experience we were offering, in what was a step into the unknown for the three of us.

Although a draftsman by training, I had been running my family's pen shop business. Daphne Swann was a close friend and colleague there. My wife, Kay Canter, was busy looking after our three young children. So, as hundreds of visitors to Cranks have asked us, "How did you begin?"

Although Kay, Daphne, and I are equal partners, they agree that it was from me that the creation of Cranks came.

The first force at work was my great leaning towards sculpture, pottery, and painting that even from school years made me want to be a designer. It was from my love of craftsmanship and natural materials that the style, which is unique to Cranks, was to come. Craftsmanship such as that of calligrapher Donald Jackson, for instance, who has lettered all our brochures and signs, raises what is so often a mundane means-to-an-end to an enriching level of beauty and creativity.

The second and more direct inspiration began with a slipped disc in 1950. The complete failure of treatment requiring weeks of bed rest, hospital traction sessions, plaster jackets (with unreachable itches!), and strong pain-killing drugs left me very depressed.

At my father's suggestion, I went for treatment to a distinguished osteopath (Mr. Puttock). He spent our sessions of back manipulation re-educating me about health, including giving me several books to read. One of them was Gaylord Hauser's *Look Younger, Live Longer*. The effect was dramatic—an exciting and fascinating reversal of all Kay's and my ideas of health and disease.

We had been brought face-to-face with the fact that I was individually responsible for my health and well-being, and that a major factor in how healthy I would be was what I ate.

We were completely convinced by the obvious sense of a philosophy which stresses that nature knows best, and so the food we eat should be as near as possible to the form in which it is harvested. Only then will it still have the complex blend of ingredients that still defies complete analysis, and yet is so essential to man's health and vitality.

We lost no time in putting our new-found knowledge into practice. We ceremoniously put all our white sugar, aspirins, and other medicines down the toilet and flushed it. We were determined that our three young children should not suffer the ills we had but should be given the natural, unrefined foods that would build the good health that was their birthright.

In spite of this conviction, we might never have thought of adventuring into a restaurant if it had not been for Ronald Beesley of the College of Psychotherapeutics. Daphne had suggested he could help me with the depression after my back problem. He was an amazing man who seemed to have a link with a spiritual power beyond ordinary comprehension. He quickly revived the life force within me, and I developed a new approach to life that later made our venture much easier.

I now felt a certainty that once I had decided on a course of action springing from the right motivation, and provided I put aside fear and had confidence, even when the path was scattered with the most frightening obstacles, all would be overcome. Fear is the corrosive factor which has within it the seeds of failure.

In this frame of mind, when a vacant bakeshop came to our attention while I was converting similar premises into the first showroom of the Craftsman Potters Association in the same street, we did not hesitate. At that time, Carnaby Street was not swinging, but a street of small shops and cafés—a saddlery, a chess shop, a hardware store, tailors, and more. Rents were low.

Takings on our first day totalled £11. 17s. 1d; with such a brisk start we gladly took on Joe Doyle, a Sydney girl who came in to have a meal and then asked for a job. Joe was the first of the many wonderful staff who have worked for us—so many of whom were from Australia or New Zealand. They possessed the ideal spirit for working in Cranks by approaching the work with enthusiasm and down-to-earth commonsense. They also looked very attractive in the blue floral dresses that we have used as our uniform from the beginning.

Working at Cranks is different from the usual restaurant. Instead of the hierarchy of jobs, ours was the amateur, family-style approach. Our staff are members of a team working on first name terms with a sense of comradeship. We don't subscribe to "the customer is always right" theory; we feel that staff and customers come together as equally as host and guest. We also avoid the use of "sirs" or "madams", and we don't accept the degrading habit of tipping.

Our staff have turned their hands to all the jobs—preparing, cooking, serving, cleaning up. So have we, creating over the years associations with many special characters among staff and suppliers as problems have arisen and been solved. Nowadays, for instance, every Cranks has its own bakery. We went through many stages to achieve this, from Kay baking at home, to our staff using a domestic oven in the Carnaby Street basement kitchen, to the final discovery that Sam Mayall's flour and Doris Grant's no-knead bread recipe was the perfect combination from which the famous Cranks loaf emerged —still unchanged for the last fifteen years. Today, we produce over 400 Cranks loaves and 550 cheese buns a day, in addition to all the cakes, pastries, and savouries.

Vegetables grown organically, without synthetic chemicals, are as important to us in our principles as compost-grown wheat, though we have always found it extremely difficult to find sufficient regular suppliers. For twenty years, Graham has brought us fruit and vegetables faithfully day in, day out from the old Covent Garden Market (now Nine Elms) to make up the shortage from organic sources.

Our urgent need for a reliable supply of natural and fresh fruit yogurts led us to approach James More-Molyneux, whose ready response resulted in Loseley becoming one of the largest suppliers of additive-free yogurt and ice-cream for the whole of the south of England.

By the mid-60s Carnaby Street had become so famous for its trendy clothes stores that we had been featured as background in dozens of documentaries. We had established a rabbit warren of small, neighboring premises giving us a Salad Bar, a Juice Bar, a health food store, and a bakery, in addition to our over-crowded restaurant.

By now, we were bursting at the seams and we leapt at the opportunity in 1967 to move into larger premises in nearby Marshall Street with seating for 170 people and a large adjoining shop. This is now the Cranks home base, from where in the next decade we opened offshoots in Dartmouth, Totnes, Guildford, and Dartington.

We weren't expanding out of London just for fun, although we have only opened in places where we have felt an affinity with the area. Country sites could be opened at a much lower cost, and the property freeholds provided security for bank loans which had to make up for our shortage of capital.

Many flattering overtures from individuals and international groups to open more Cranks or even Cranks franchises at home and overseas have been declined. We have wanted to remain a relatively small concern where we could maintain tight control of food and aesthetic standards. But when Heals of Tottenham Court Road, London, and the Peter Robinson group at Oxford Circus each invited us to open up Cranks restaurants which allowed us our own style and control, we did. The exception is the Cranks Grønne Buffet, opened in 1979 by Daniel and Yette Hage in Copenhagen. Because of the distance, our annual visit to them gives us a rare chance to sit together quietly and take a bird's eye view of everything we are doing at Cranks.

It has always been a basic principle of ours that each Cranks should be a self-sufficient unit. However small, it must have its own bakery to produce bread, savouries, and cakes. This is not only to simplify organization and avoid delivery services but, more importantly, it gives each branch a sense of wholeness and job satisfaction because the staff can be totally involved.

A problem that is constantly with us is how to pitch our prices and decide how much we can afford to pay in salaries. There are many people who think that because we own and run a business with a turnover of over £2 million a year we must be wealthy. This is far from the case!

We were lucky enough to receive some very sound basic advice from our accountants before we opened. They suggested we multiplied our food costs by three to arrive at the menu price and kept our salaries within 25 per cent of takings (it is currently between 28 and 30%). We have stuck to this over the years, and those of our customers who may think our prices too high are, with the greatest respect, unaware of the specially high cost of our kind of operation.

Although they are right in thinking that our choice of buffet service requires fewer staff, far more are required behind the scenes than at most restaurants. Because we make every dish fresh daily from basic ingredients, there is a vast amount of washing, chopping, and preparing that other restaurants avoid, often using ready-made mixes and pre-packaged vegetables instead.

Our ingredients are also more expensive than the catering norm. A notable example is our use of free-range eggs only, when we could use powdered eggs from battery farms at a fraction of the price. The pleasure of eating from handthrown stoneware, in our view, outweighs the thousands of pounds spent a year replacing it. Our customers must like it–they have always tended to take some home with them!

Each partner has played a different role. Daphne has become a very effective businesswoman, responsible for the day-to-day affairs of purchasing, employing, and control of staff, and many of the other facets in keeping Cranks running smoothly. One of Daphne's qualities has been her ability to be in sympathy with the staff in a way that brings out the best in them and helps the team feeling. She can also get her teeth into a problem and see it through.

Kay has gradually been able to give more time to the business as our children have grown up. Her devotion to 'good housekeeping'– standards of food, cleanliness, and service–is so strong as to be creative, not in any way secondary. It is Kay who keeps Cranks in touch with animal protection and anti-pollution societies, so that their leaflets and concerns come to the attention of thousands of our customers.

As to myself, I can claim to be the innovator and designer with the imagination and will to bring new projects into being. As chairman, mine is the ultimate responsibility for our financial needs and problems, although in practice most of the decisions are agreed between the three of us.

It must be very unusual for three people to agree so often. It happens because we have very similar ideas about what Cranks should be like. As we approach our sixties, we wonder about our future and that of those combined beliefs that became the institution of Cranks.

So many people ask us why we chose the name "Cranks." It was not because we considered ourselves, as the dictionary puts it, "faddists", but because we wanted a label to show that with strong vegetarian and whole food principles, we were very different from the orthodox retail and catering establishment, and we wanted a light-hearted, humorous approach.

Nowadays healthy eating is no longer seen as "cranky"–perhaps we are seen as unusual for our tenacity in sticking to the best ingredients, labor-intensive methods, and craftsman-made surroundings despite their soaring costs.

These are things worth fighting for, and fortunately our many supporters show they enjoy them as much as we do. Cranks couldn't exist without the support of those who work for us–now some 200 people–and those who eat with us. That sense of community is another element of the lovely spirit of Cranks. Tasting is believing!

List of recipes

Soup

Bran water & oatmeal water to
   use as stock
Creamy onion soup
Green pea soup
Cream of watercress soup
Mangetout soup
Borscht
Cream of leek soup
Cream of spinach & zucchini
   soup
Fresh tomato soup
Apple & peanut butter soup
Mushroom soup
Mulligatawny soup
Creamy potato soup
Carrot potage
Buckwheat & potato soup
Carrot, apple & cashew nut
   soup
Armenian soup
Egg & lemon soup
Cheddar cheese soup
Celery & cashew nut soup
Parsnip & apple soup
Cauliflower soup
Potage Malakoff
Russian vegetable soup
Pumpkin & spinach soup
French onion soup
Country vegetable soup
Lentil & tomato soup
Chunky bean soup
Hauser soup
Gazpacho

Salads

Carrot mayonnaise
Coleslaw
Cucumber in tarragon dressing
Waldorf salad
Spinach & mushroom salad
Beet, celery & orange salad
Potato salad
Carrot & rutabaga in sour
   cream dressing
Celery & apple salad
Whole wheat mayonnaise
Hawaiian rice salad
Creamy beet salad
Leek salad
Italian pasta salad
Bulghur salad
Celery, cucumber & grape
   salad
Cauliflower, date & banana
   salad
Green pepper & orange salad
Alfalfa salad
Taboullah
Endive & oranges with cheese
   dressing
Green bean salad
Green salad
Tomato salad
Flageolet bean salad
Beansprout salad
Cabbage & orange salad
Cucumber, tomato & cheese
   salad
Watercress & carrot salad
Avocado salad
Sweet & sour radishes
Lentil sprout salad
Spiced pepper salad
Turmeric rice salad
Ploughman's salad
Tangy zucchini salad
Tzatziki salad

Starters

Tamari cashews
Hummus
Garlic relish
Mushroom pâté
Cream cheese & cashew nut
   pâté
Wine & nut pâté
Egg & tomato mousse
Baked grapefruit (I & II)
Florida salad
Mushrooms à la grecque
Ratatouille
Stuffed tomatoes
Creamy baked tomatoes
Tarragon eggs en cocotte
Eggs Indienne
Egg mayonnaise
Nut cheese
Sava
Soy cheese

Dressings & sauces

Savouries

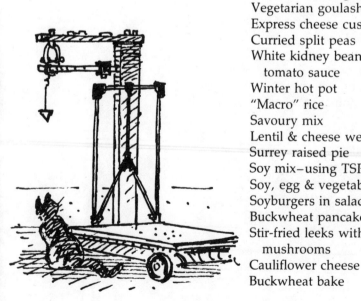

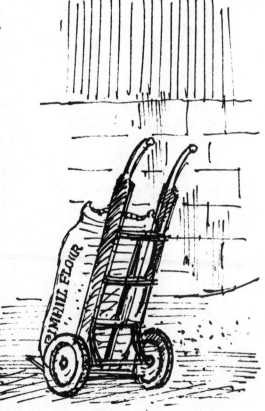

Biscuits

Cranks flapjack
Melting moments
Eccles cakes
Date slices
Carob crunch
Shortbread
Country biscuits
Coconut biscuits
Carob chip cookies
Florentines
Sesame thins
Millet & peanut cookies
Caraway bran biscuits
Crunchies
Peanut rounds
Gingernuts
Cheesejacks
Cheese biscuits
Whole wheat rusks
Melba toast

Breakfast cereals

Breakfast cereal
Muesli
Milled whole wheat berries
    & nuts

Bread

Cranks whole wheat bread
Corn & molasses bread
Rye bread
Bran bread
Barley bread
Soy bread
Sourdough bread
Cheese bread
Garlic bread
Cheese buns
Herb bread
Granary loaf
Four-grain bread
Pumpernickel
Unyeasted bread
Oatmeal soda bread
Apple & banana bread
Spiced currant bread
Walnut tea bread
Hot cross buns
Jam doughnuts
Chelsea buns

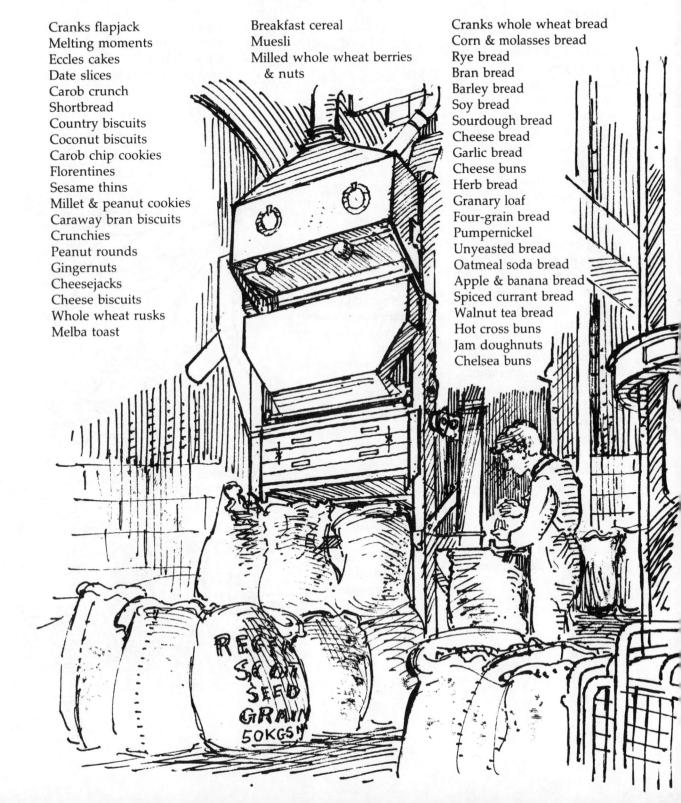

Puddings & desserts

Creamy yogurt pie
Banana yogurt pie
Puréed fruit gelatin
Lemon cheesecake
Lemon meringue pie
Sticky prune cake
Raw sugar jam tart
Baked egg custard
Orange & banana trifle
Creamy bran & apple chunks
Apple pie
Bakewell tart
Spiced bread pudding
Tangy apple swirl
Grape & banana pie
Junket
"Toffeed" rhubarb fool
Custard tart
Walnut pie
Hazelnut & black cherry tart
Carrageenan citrus gelatin
Devon apple cake
Carob blancmange
Brandied prune mousse
Buttermilk dessert
Honey & apple tart
Date & apple squares
Molasses tart
Apple crumble
Bread & butter pudding
Baked apples
Pouding Alsace
Mincemeat & apple "jalousie"
Home-made yogurt
Christmas pudding

Cakes & scones

Belgian cake
Old-fashioned ginger cake
100% whole wheat sponge
Jelly roll
Christmas cake
Almond paste
Mock marzipan
Raw sugar icing
Luscious lemon cake
Carob cake
Date & coconut gâteau
Carrot cake
Honey cake
Poppyseed cake
Walnut sandwich cake
Simnel cake
Orange cake
Date & walnut loaf
Orange ginger cake
Fruit cake without eggs
Barabrith
Whole wheat muffins
Bran muffins
Apple cakes
Old English rock buns
Raspberry buns
Walnut bars
Chocolate éclairs
Fruit scones
Drop scones
Cheese scones
Raw sugar meringues
Welsh butter cakes
Coconut castles
Honey buns
Truffle triangle

Pastry

Whole wheat shortcrust pastry
Hot water crust pastry
Choux pastry
Whole wheat pastry made with
  oil

Preserves & sweets

Coarse-cut orange marmalade
Lemon curd
Apple butter
Apple & ginger chutney
Fruit & nut chews
Marzipan shapes
Coconut bars
Carob fudge
Dried apricot & almond jam

Drinks

Freshly extracted vegetable & fruit juices
Preparation for extracted juices
Recipes for drinks as served at Cranks

Culinary know-how

What you need to know about health foods and their preparation before you start to cook.

Flours & pasta

100% Whole grain flour. This is flour in nature's complete form, with all the valuable vitamins, minerals, and trace elements contained in the outer husk (bran) and central wheat germ, as well as the protein and starch content. The best whole grain flour is that which has been milled by stone (stoneground) rather than by the steel rollers used by the large millers, and which has been grown organically, without the use of chemical fertilizers.

In Cranks bakeries we use only 100% whole wheat flour in all our products, except of course for barley and rye bread. Although our Cranks Health Loaf is made in such a way as to achieve the close, moist texture of the Grant Loaf, the method has to be geared to large production.

85% Whole wheat flour. To arrive at an 85% flour the whole grain is milled in such a way as to remove most of the bran, amounting to 15% of the bulk. This produces a finer and paler flour of less nutritional value than 100% but nevertheless of very much greater value than white flour that has had most of its food value removed and has also been adulterated with chemical additives to achieve a high degree of whiteness.

Soy flour. Made from the ground soy bean, this is a fine, pale flour. It is a rich protein source, and can be added to wheat bread dough to give additional food value and to help keep it moist. It can also be used to make mock marzipan *(see page 139)* and Bakewell tart *(see page 124)*.

Rye flour. Made from milled rye grains, it may be dark or light depending on the removal of bran. It is most suitable for bread doughs, although rye bread will be flatter than wheat because of the lower gluten content. Rye flour is rich in vitamins and minerals, with a 12% protein content, and is low in gluten.

23

Barley flour. Made from milled barley grains, it is very pale in color and fine textured. It is normally used in conjunction with wheat flour and is suitable for bread and biscuits and to thicken sauces.

Cornmeal. Corn kernels are ground to a coarse or fine pale yellow meal. Use as a thickening agent or in breads and puddings.

Rice flour. Unpolished or brown rice is milled and ground to produce fine, medium, or coarse flours. Use in biscuits or as a thickening agent.

Gluten-free flour. Gluten-free flours are available for those on special diets.

Buckwheat flour. Ground buckwheat produces a fine, dark, speckled flour. Used particularly in batters.

Whole wheat pasta. Available in a wide range of shapes, this is made from 100% whole wheat flour or buckwheat flour.

Cereals & grains

Barley. The chief bread grain of the Hebrews, Greeks, and Romans, and of much of Europe until modern times. Pearl barley has had the outer layers and germ removed, while pot barley has had only the indigestible husk removed.

Wheat. This has been the principal cereal grain of Europe and the Near East for thousands of years. Modern wheats are of three main types:

Bread wheats are high in gluten-forming proteins.

Soft wheats are low in gluten and give a light texture to cakes, biscuits, and pastry.

Durum wheats are the hardest and are used to make pasta products. Whole wheat berries add a mild, nutty flavor to soups and stews and make an ideal base for salads and breakfast cereals. Flaked wheat is also available.

Oats. Higher in protein and oil than other grains, oats were originally wild plants considered to be weeds. They were then domesticated and used in the harsh climate of northern Europe and are well suited to our cold, damp English winters. Oats are more commonly used as oatmeal, which is the whole grain rolled or cut into flakes, available in fine, medium, and coarse meal.

Rye. This hardy grain is often cultivated where high altitudes, cold temperatures, or poor soil discourages other grains. In Eastern Europe rye flour is particularly popular, but less so in Britain.

Buckwheat. Not a grain but the seeds of the plant sometimes known as Saracen corn. Rich in protein and minerals, it contains most of the vitamin B complex. Also available ready-roasted.

Millet. Dating back to prehistoric times, millet is richer in vitamins, mineral, and fat content than any other grain. The grain has its protective, uneatable husk removed before use. It has a high protein content and is easily digested. Also available as flakes.

Bulghur. A preparation of wheat used in Middle Eastern cooking. It is made by cooking wheat, then drying and cracking it. Bulghur comes in varying degrees of coarseness and has excellent nutritional value as a good source of phosphorus, iron, and B vitamins.

Rice. This has been a staple food for thousands of years in Asia, China, Spain, and Italy and is grown extensively in the East, as well as France, Eastern Europe, Australia, and the USA. It is the largest food crop in the world. Rice is similar in structure to wheat and goes through a process of milling that removes the outer husk, leaving a brownish grain that is the bran-covered rice. This bran is removed to give white rice (known as polished rice). Whole (brown) rice retains all the valuable minerals and vitamins and is a good source of starch. Its protein content is lower than that of other grains. Brown rice takes a little longer to cook than white rice and has a delicious nutty flavor. Adding some oil or a pat of butter to the water in which the rice is boiled avoids the tendency of the rice to cook into a coagulated mass.

Wheat germ. As the name implies, this is the actual germ of the wheat, the part from which the new plant springs. The most nutritious wheat germ is unstabilized, but it follows that it has a more limited shelf life than the stabilized product. It is an extremely valuable source of vitamin E, as well as part of the vitamin B complex and minerals, including iron. Its main value is the yield of vitamin E that can be obtained in the form of oil.

Bran. The protective, tough outer cover of the wheat grain. It is milled together with the rest of the grain to make 100% whole wheat flour, but can also be separated from the grain and used as supplementary roughage in the diet. It is a rich source of protein, vitamin B complex, and phosphorus and is valued for its high fiber content.

Cornstarch. This is the white starch extracted from the rhizome of a herbaceous perennial plant, indigenous in West Indian islands and possibly Central America. It is now grown in Bengal, Java, the Philippines, Mauritius, Natal, and West Africa. It is used as a thickening agent and is considered to be useful in remedying digestive disorders.

Legumes & beans

Lentils. These are grown in the Mediterranean region and were used in early days by the Greeks and Egyptians. The seeds are dried, dehusked and sometimes split and are either orange-red or greenish-brown in color. They have a high protein content and are quite easily digested.

Chickpeas. A legume crop of India, now grown in America, Africa, and Australia. Creamy yellow in color and mealy in texture when cooked. A good source of protein.

Dried beans. These are rich in iron, potassium, and vitamin B complex and low in carbohydrate and fat. They also contain a high fiber content and so provide essential roughage within the diet.

There are many different types of bean available. These include:

Flageolets. Pale green in color with an elongated bean shape.

Red kidney beans. Dark red in color.

WARNING: It has recently been discovered that there is a poisonous substance in red kidney beans that is only destroyed when they are fast boiled for at least 10 minutes.

Split peas. Split dried peas with the skin removed.

White kidney beans (navy beans). White in color, a fairly small bean.

All these beans must be soaked before cooking.
Cooking times will vary according to type and age.
Do not add salt during boiling as this will toughen the skins.

Seeds

Sesame. Grown mainly in Africa, Asia, and South America, these seeds are white or brown in color. The seeds contain almost 50% oil, are high in protein, and are a good source of vitamin B complex and minerals, particularly calcium.

Sunflower. Grown mainly in Russia and the USA, they are particularly rich in vitamin B complex and a good source of minerals and protein.

Caraway. A plant native to the Mediterranean shores but now indigenous all over Europe. Grown largely for its aromatic seeds.

Alfalfa. A plant rich in protein and minerals, including iron, calcium and magnesium, and a source of vitamins B12 and K.

Some seeds, such as mung beans, alfalfa, and lentils, can be easily sprouted at home in jars and are ready to eat in 3-6 days. They are a valuable source of fresh vitamins all year round. Sprouting seeds can be bought from health food stores.

Dried fruits

Dried fruits are rich in natural sugar (fructose) and are often much sweeter than their fresh counterpart because the fruits are left on the trees to ripen for a greater length of time. They are also rich in minerals such as potassium and iron and vitamins A and B. Processing techniques vary, but usually the fruit is picked, halved, pitted, or left whole according to type, and then dried. Sun drying is the most suitable method of drying, but artificial heat is sometimes used. Other methods include the use of sulphur dioxide or freeze-drying.

Apricots. These contain a considerable amount of vitamin C and A. First grown in Northern Asia, they are now imported from South Africa, Australia, and Turkey. Color and flavor vary with country of origin.

Dates. Available with or without the pit, dates are imported from North Africa and California. Eaten both fresh and dry, they are a wonderful instance of nature's sweetening, containing vitamins A, B1, and B2. An easily digested energy food.

Prunes. They are high in vitamins A and B. The best plums for drying are Santa Clara, which are American but are also imported from South America and Australia.

Currants. These are the dried fruit of a tiny purple grape that are sharper in flavor than sultanas or raisins. They are mainly imported from Greece.

Raisins. Known since Biblical times, they are rich in iron and copper, and available in two sorts: pitted or seeded (when the pits have been removed) and seedless (from grapes that have no seeds). Pitted raisins are larger and considered superior. Raisins are imported from Spain, Australia, America, and South Africa.

Sultanas. They come from a seedless grape, are much sweeter than either currants or raisins, and should be light in color and fleshy. They are imported from Australia, South Africa, Turkey, and parts of the Mediterranean. They are called yellow, or golden raisins in the USA.

All dried fruits should be thoroughly washed before using.

Nuts

Almond. The kernel of the fruit of the almond tree, widely grown in California.

Brazil nut. The fruit of a large tree, grown originally in Brazil–hence the name. The segment-like nuts fit together in a similar way to an orange and are encased in an outer husk like a coconut shell.

Cashew nut. The kidney-shaped seeds of a tropical tree native to Brazil but now grown in India and East Africa. The fruit is like a large fleshy apple and has a nut hanging below it containing the kernel, which is manually extracted after roasting.

Chestnut. Large brown nut of a native Mediterranean tree.

Coconut. The fruit of the coconut palm, consisting of the inner husk containing the white coconut and milk. It originated in Malaya but is now grown in most tropical regions of the world. The white flesh is dried and grated to made dried coconut.

Walnut. The fruit of the walnut tree. The walnut has a smooth, outer green husk that is removed when the ripe nuts are picked. The outer shell is removed and only the kernel is eaten.

Peanut. Sometimes known as the ground nut, it is not a true nut but comes in the pod of a leguminous plant, which grows underground. There are two kernels in each pod. Peanuts are grown extensively in Africa and South America.

Sugar, sweeteners & preserves

Raw sugar. Raw sugar is a natural product from unrefined cane sugar. It does not contain any artificial coloring or additives of any sort. Raw sugar is always produced in the country of origin, and if this is not stated on the package it is not the "real" thing. In the U.K., it comes in four types:

Demerara. This has clear, sparkling crystals of a large, consistent size. It also has a crunchy yet sticky texture and rich aroma because of its natural molasses. It takes its name from Demerara, Guyana, where it was first produced. Its nearest U.S. equivalent is turbinado sugar. *Dark brown sugar.* Sometimes called Barbados sugar, this is a soft, sticky, fine-grained, dark brown sugar, rich in natural molasses.

Light brown sugar. A creamy-colored soft cane sugar.

Molasses sugar. Also known as Black Barbados or Demerara Molasses. Stronger in flavor than brown sugar because of the greater molasses content, it is sticky and almost black and is very rich in minerals and trace elements.

Store raw sugars in a lidded jar. If the sugar becomes solid, add a small piece of cut raw potato to the storage jar or place the package of sugar in a plastic bag with the piece of cut raw potato and seal it. Before using it in cooking always pick over the sugar to remove any large lumps. Alternatively, push it through a sieve or blend in a blender.

Molasses. A thick, dark syrup left over when sugar cane is refined. Molasses is a good source of vitamin B and is particularly rich in iron.

Honey. A natural product made from the nectar of flowers. Bees collect the nectar and its structure of sugars is processed by the enzymes present in the bee's stomach. It is then stored in the honeycomb where the sugar conversion continues to produce the product known as honey, which is a fragile, delicately balanced mixture of carbohydrates in water, with fat, protein, enzymes, vitamins, amino acids, and aromatic compounds. The flavor of each honey will vary with the differing balance of these constituents, the flowers from which the nectar was collected, the weather, and natural variation.

Honey is very easily digested and so is a good, quick source of energy. It can be used in place of sugar as a sweetening agent, but care must be taken when using it in cake mixtures as it has a strong and distinctive flavor, so follow a recipe.

Other natural sweeteners such as maple syrup, rice bran syrup, and barley malt also make good sugar substitutes. Because of the different consistencies and flavors of these sweeteners, it is best to follow a recipe when using them, especially for baking.

Preserves. Jams, sweet mincemeat, and marmalade can be made with raw sugar and are available from health food stores. See recipes in the Preserves chapter.

Oils

These are an essential part of the diet. They contain acids (essential fatty acids) that cannot be manufactured by the body and must be provided in the diet. They play a significant part in cell structure and can assist in the remedy of skin ailments. They contain vitamins A, D, E, and K. Most health stores concentrate on the sale of sunflower, safflower, and corn oils. These all contain a high percentage of polyunsaturated fatty acids, which make them desirable for use in diets where coronary disease is a consideration or preventative measures are necessary. Peanut and olive oils are not suitable for this purpose. Soy oil is of limited value but is a protein source. Sesame oil is also available.

Unrefined oils are the first choice of health-conscious people because they consist of the first 30% of oil extracted from the seeds, beans, or grains by cold pressing. The residual mash left from the pressing then has some 70% of its weight extracted as oil by being dissolved in a chemical solvent that is later removed.

Butter

This is produced from milk and usually contains more than 80% butterfat. It also contains vitamins A and D and small amounts of protein, milk sugar, and minerals.

Margarine

Look for margarine that is made from pure vegetable oils and is suitable for vegans. Many margarines may contain a mixture of marine, animal, and vegetable oils and possibly whey, so are not suitable for a strict vegetarian diet.

Cheese

Cottage cheese. This is a type of curd cheese made from skim milk with the addition of rennet. The resulting curds are cut and washed to produce the familiar granular and creamy texture. Cream is often added for a richer product.

Curd cheese. This soft, smooth cheese can be made by simply allowing the milk to "turn" naturally, but it is more usually made by adding a lactic starter to the milk. The resulting curds and whey are separated, and the curds become known as curd cheese. The closest U.S. equivalent is Ricotta or farmer's cheese.

Cream cheese. This is made by a similar process to that for curd cheese, but cream and not milk is used as the basic ingredient. The cream is cultured with either a lactic starter or a rennet, and the resulting curds and whey are strained to give cream cheese. It is obviously richer than curd and cottage cheeses.

Skim milk cheese. Skim milk is milk that has had the cream removed from it and is therefore virtually free from fat. Curd cheese made from this is highly favored in a healthy and reducing diet.

Hard cheeses, e.g., Cheddar, Double Gloucester. Hard cheeses made with a vegetarian rennet, as opposed to an animal rennet, are available in most health food stores.

Cream, milk & yogurt

Sour cream. This is actually cultured and not soured. Light cream is treated in a similar way to milk when making yogurt by adding a "live" cheese culture to it.

Fresh dairy cream. This may be untreated, in which case it should be bought and used as quickly as possible.

Pasteurized cream has undergone heat-treatment, a process that destroys bacteria and prolongs its keeping qualities but also reduces its nutritional value. It is available as light, heavy, or whipping. The thickness of cream varies with the butterfat content.

Skim milk. This is milk with enough of the cream content "skimmed" off to leave a fat content of less than 0.2%.

Skim milk powder. Milk powder is produced by the evaporation of water from milk by heat, or other means, to produce solids containing 5% or less moisture. Skim milk powder contains virtually no fat, and therefore no fat-soluble vitamins, but it does contain protein, calcium, and riboflavin.

Yogurt. This is produced from milk by the introduction of two organisms–*Lactobacillus bulgaricus* and *Streptococcus thermophilus*–which cause fermentation of the lactic acid within the milk. When a carton of yogurt indicates that the contents are "live", this means that the bacillus bulgaricus remains active within the yogurt with a resulting beneficial effect on the digestive processes assisted by the production of vitamin B within the body. It is an excellent source of protein and provides a significant quantity of calcium, so always buy "live" yogurt ready to eat or to use as a starter for home-made yogurt (see page 132).

Buttermilk. There are two sorts of buttermilk:

(a)   The liquid left over when butter is produced from milk.

(b)   A cultured milk made from separated milk. The method is similar to that of yogurt-making. A culture is introduced to the milk, which is then heated. The resulting buttermilk is much thicker than type (a).

Soy milk. This is "milk" produced from soy flour and is therefore valuable for vegans as an alternative to cows' milk.

Hypo-allergenic soy infant formula is fiber-free and well-balanced in protein, soy fat, and carbohydrates. It is easily digested and can be used as an alternative to cows' milk.

Cider vinegar

This is considered by naturopaths and other experts to be more beneficial to health than either malt or wine vinegar. To some extent this view seems to emerge from the folk medicine tradition. Undoubtedly cider vinegar is rich in the mineral salts, particularly potassium, and these have a very beneficial effect on the body's metabolism. It is thought that the combination of the acetic acid produced by the conversion of the cider into vinegar, and the citric acid from the apples, quickly metabolizes in the body and so produces a significant alkaline increase and therefore an improvement in the vital alkaline/acid balance in the bloodstream. This is helpful in many disorders of the body, particularly arthritis. The cider vinegar used in Cranks comes from Áspall Hall in Suffolk and is made from organically grown apples.

Soy sauce

The use and manufacture of soy sauce has been known in China since the sixth century. There may be some confusion between the various types of soy sauce on the market. Tamari is a term that has been used to describe soy sauce that is naturally fermented and made without the use of chemicals. Soy sauce is made from a mixture of wheat and soybeans, which has been soaked until soft, slightly cooked with water and sea salt, and then inoculated with "koji" bacteria to promote fermentation. The mixture is allowed to ferment and is then aged During the curing, the sauce is occasionally stirred to ensure even fermentation. After the mash is pressed and the liquid extracted, the soy sauce is quickly heated to slow down the fermentation and preserve the flavor.

TSP (Textured soy protein)

This is a processed soy bean product used in vegetarian cooking as an alternative source of protein. It is available in dehydrated form as "mince" or in chunks. This is sold under various trade names and stocked in most health food stores.

Natural extracts

A whole range of natural extracts is available from health food stores. These extracts are completely free of synthetic substances. Flavors include almond, vanilla, ginger, and peppermint.

Jelling compounds *(The vegetarian alternative to gelatin, which is derived from animal carcasses).*

Carrageenan. A particular type of seaweed that can be bought in packages in a dried form and used for thickening stews, soups, jellies, and so on. Follow the instructions on the package.

Gelozone. A starch-free jelling agent made from a special preparation of Irish moss and Carrageenan moss. Used to thicken hot drinks, soups, and sauces.

Agar-agar. A jelling compound derived from seaweed, which produces a cloudy jelly, not a clear one as with the usual packaged variety of tablet gelatin.

Carob

Carob beans are the fruit of the carob tree, usually found in warm climates such as Spain, Greece, Cyprus, Italy and Morocco. They look like dark brown, shiny string beans but are very hard. The ripe pods are crushed and the pulpy portion of the beans is separated from the hard seeds. This is ground to a powder, which may be substituted in any recipe that calls for cocoa or chocolate powder. It is also available in a bar as an alternative to chocolate. Although processed carob and chocolate look alike and taste alike, carob is more than a mere substitute. It is rich in vitamins and minerals and, unlike chocolate, contains no refined sugar or habit-forming caffeine.

Rennet

Vegetarian rennet is available for making cheese and junket. It is made from a microbial enzyme, and in some cases from an extract of French mushrooms. (Animal rennet is derived from the stomach of a calf.)

Vegetable stock cubes

Available with or without salt, these are made from vegetable fat, yeast extract, lactose, hydrolized vegetable protein, sunflower oil, vegetables, and spices.

Yeast

A great variety of yeasts exist in nature as living cells, and some are specially suited for yeast cooking. These selected and specially bred strains of yeast are isolated and cultivated scientifically and sold as compressed yeast. This active yeast is also dried in such a way that the cells will remain active after many months of storage in a cool place. This is dried baking yeast and is usually sold in small packages. Dried yeast can be used instead of fresh yeast and is equally successful for bread making. Always follow the instructions on the package on how to reconstitute or incorporate the dried yeast into the flour.

There are also other kinds of dried yeast that are inactive and will not raise bread. These have a valuable source of vitamin B which, in a powdered or flaked form, may be sprinkled over cereals, added to baked goods, such as bread, or consumed in tablet form as a dietary supplement.

Brewer's yeast. This is a by-product of the brewing process and is sold in powdered and tablet form. It has been found to contain seventeen vitamins, including all the B vitamins and fourteen minerals, including the essential trace elements. It also contains 36% protein.

Yeast extract (Vegex). When brewer's yeast is mixed with salt it is broken down by its own enzymes. The soluble residue is evaporated to produce yeast extract, familiar as a sticky brown substance. There are a number of different brands available, varying in flavor with individual ingredients. The best one is made from a vegetable concentrate, containing seaweed, which is rich in minerals.

Preparation of fruit & vegetables for cooking

In most fruit and vegetables the vitamins and minerals are stored in or just below the skin. For this reason, at Cranks we do not peel fruit or vegetables but simply wash or scrub them. However, there are obvious exceptions such as onions and garlic that need to be skinned, and fruit like bananas and pineapple that must be peeled.

In some cases, as when making purées, it is preferable to remove outer skins. There is no need to throw these peelings away–both vegetable and fruit peelings should be reserved. They can then be simmered separately in water, strained, covered, and stored in a refrigerator to use as needed. Vegetable water can be used as stock or as a base for drinks, while fruit-flavored water can be used to make a fruit syrup for salad, used as a drink, or can be set with jelling compound. Citrus fruit peel, or halves, should be kept and dried out in the oven. To do this, place the fruit halves cut-side down on a baking sheet. Place in a cool oven and leave for several hours until completely moisture free. Crumble the peel into small pieces and grind in a coffee mill. Sift and store the resulting powder in an airtight container, and use to add to cakes, biscuits, puddings, and so on to give added flavor.

The quantity of fruit and vegetables in all recipes indicates their weight prior to preparation. They must then be scrubbed, washed or trimmed, as necessary, ready for use, as follows:

apples, pears, etc.	wash and core
plums, grapes, apricots, etc.	wash, remove pits or seeds
banana, pineapple, etc.	peel or cut away the skin
citrus fruits	peel and cut away white pith if wished
root vegetables	scrub and trim
leafy vegetables and herbs	wash and discard any discolored leaves
peppers	cut in half, discard stem, and remove seeds
mushrooms	wash or wipe, do not peel
celery	separate sticks, scrub and trim
leeks	trim, clean thoroughly to remove soil

Herbs

Whenever possible use fresh herbs in cooking. Simply wash and dry the herb to be used and chop it. When using dried herbs, do remember that the flavor is more concentrated and a lesser amount should be added. Dried herbs may be reconstituted in a little warm water before use.

The use of salt & pepper in the cooking & preparation of food

Salt. Ordinary table or common salt is almost pure sodium chloride, which could cause an imbalance if taken in the quantities given in the recipes. At Cranks we recommend that you use only sea salt. We also suggest that you follow the quantities of salt in the recipes carefully and make a note of any adjustment you might want to make to suit your taste.

Pepper. Black pepper is a whole berry. The outer husk of the ripe berry is removed to produce white peppercorns. These are both ground to give the resulting black and white peppers.

The use of a minute timer

All the recipes in this book have been tested and their cooking times checked. Although there may be slight variations in temperature with different types of ovens, it is always advisable to use a timer when following a recipe.

Oven temperature guide

	Electric °F
Very cool	225–250
Cool	275–300
Warm	325
Moderate	350
Fairly hot	375–400
Hot	425
Very hot	450–475

Freezing of food

Specific instructions for freezing are not included in this book, but this does not mean that particular recipes are unsuitable for freezing.

There are many good books available on this subject that will supply all the necessary details on suitability of foods for freezing and how to package them. As a general rule, breads and baked goods freeze particularly well–soups and savouries too, providing they do not contain cream. Flavorings, especially garlic, are affected by freezing, which considerably reduces their storage time to a maximum of three weeks.

Cooking terms

To bake "blind." Baking pastry cases without a filling. To do this, cut a circle of waxed paper about 2 in. larger than the pastry shell and place this inside the pastry shell. Fill with dried beans and bake as per recipe. Keep the beans for future use.

To pare. Referring to citrus fruit rind. To remove the outer zest of the fruit in a thin strip. This is most easily done with a potato peeler or small sharp knife.

To toast. Referring to dried coconut or cereals. Lay the coconut or cereal on a shallow baking sheet and brown, turning frequently, under a medium hot broiler or in a fairly hot oven until evenly golden.

To whisk. Adding one ingredient to another to produce an evenly combined mixture, or incorporating air into a mixture, i.e., into egg whites for meringues, using either a fork, whisk, or electric mixer.

To dice. To cut into small cubes.

To shred. To slice finely using a sharp knife or coarse grater.

To hard boil. Referring to eggs. Place eggs in a saucepan of boiling water and simmer gently 10 minutes. Plunge immediately into cold water and allow to cool before removing the shell.

To steam. Usually of fruit, vegetables, and sometimes bread. A method of cooking utilizing the steam from boiling water. This can be done in a steamer or in a bowl inside a saucepan of water.

To sauté. Usually referring to vegetables. To fry quickly in a minimum of oil, stirring frequently to prevent sticking.

To crush. Referring to garlic. Peel garlic clove and either push through a garlic press or place on a chopping board, sprinkle with a little salt, and, using the flat side of a knife blade, squash the garlic to a paste.

Referring to biscuits. Place biscuits in a plastic bag and reduce to crumbs with a rolling pin.

To blend. To purée in a blender until smooth. Care should be taken that the food is cool before blending, otherwise a build-up of steam will produce a vacuum and the lid will blow off!

To make whole wheat breadcrumbs. Cut stale whole wheat bread into small pieces and rub through a sieve or reduce to crumbs in a blender.

To toast crumbs, spread the fresh breadcrumbs on a shallow baking sheet and toast under a medium hot broiler, turning occasionally, or dry out in a moderate oven until crisp.

To blanch. To plunge food into boiling water, usually to preserve its natural color, to remove a flavor that is too strong or to soften the texture of the food.

To marinate. To soak food in a blend of liquids such as oil, vinegar or lemon juice, and seasonings to give flavor to that food.

To "top and tail." Referring to vegetables such as beans or radishes. To trim them at each end to remove stalks, leaves, etc.

To rise. Referring to yeasted doughs. To leave dough in a warm place, covered with oiled plastic wrap until the dough has doubled in size or until it has reached the top of the pan.

To knead. Usually of bread dough or pastry. To work the dough by hand, or using the dough hook of an electric mixer, in a continuous circular movement, to produce a smooth dough. In the case of bread dough, kneading is essential to ensure an even texture throughout the finished bread.

To fold in. To incorporate two mixtures carefully together using a large metal spoon, or spatula, in a figure-eight movement. This is usually required when adding an ingredient or mixture to another mixture that is highly aerated to prevent excessive loss of air and consequent lightness in the finished dish, e.g., adding flour to a whisked egg and sugar mixture when making a whisked egg sponge.

Containers to cook in

There is evidence to suggest that there is a poisonous release from aluminum cooking vessels that causes harmful reactions in the body. Cranks strongly recommends the use of stainless steel or good quality enamel or iron in place of aluminum. See the Bibliography (*page 41*) for a book with more information on this subject.

Pressure cookers. Pressure cooking is a quick and efficient method of cooking, but just because it is so fast it is very necessary to time carefully to avoid overcooking. It is possible to get stainless steel pressure cookers.

Steamers. It is surprising that cooking in a steamer is a method not more commonly used. In Cranks we are very much in favor of this method because it ensures that the maximum goodness and flavor is retained within the food.

Petal steamers, which are adjustable to fit various sizes of saucepan, are widely available and can be very useful, particularly for fruit and vegetables. Conventional steamers can be used very effectively for the cooking of puddings and specialized breads.

Bibliography

From the huge variety of books now written on health, diet, and nutrition, we have singled out a few special ones, some of which we feel have now become classics in their own right. A number of the books may not always be available and in such instances we suggest you refer to your local library.

Silent Spring by Rachel Carson
A passionate scientific exposure of the effects of the indiscriminate use of insecticides on wildlife and on the balance of nature–and of man's progressive poisoning of his own habitat.

Look Younger, Live Longer by Gaylord Hauser
A book full of valuable advice from this famous nutritionist, revealing his secrets for good food, good health, and good looks.

Your Daily Food (A Recipe for Survival) by Doris Grant
Well-documented and convincing, this book explains fully the hazards and dangers of modern living and the decline in our food that has become increasingly contaminated, and offers practical advice on how to avoid them.

Animal Machines by Ruth Harrison
A penetrating indictment on intensive factory farming methods.

Small is Beautiful by Dr. E. F. Schumacher
"Economics as if people mattered." The book that has earned Dr. Schumacher such world-wide recognition. It provides an important basis to Schumacher's thinking and is a guide to the main issues that concerned him, such as appropriate technology, energy policies, industrial ownership, and organization.

Back to Eden by Jethro Kloss
A classic guide to herbal medicine, natural foods, and home remedies.

The Biochemic Handbook
An introduction to the cellular therapy and practical application of the 12 tissue cell-salts in accordance with the biochemical system of medicine originated by Dr. W. H. Schuessler.

Stalking the Wild Asparagus by Euell Gibbons
A field guide to edible wild plants.

Nature Cure in a Nutshell by Tom W. Moule
A small, concise handbook of practical hints for healthful living
based on nature cure and diet reform principles.

Arthritis and Folk Medicine by D. C. Jarvis
Common sense practical suggestions for helping to relieve arthritis
and allied complaints, based on nature's laws.

Cooking for Special Diets by Bee Nilson
A comprehensive guide for providing meals for those on special
diets.

Having a Baby Easily by Margaret Brady
Practical advice on all aspects of child care, with dietary advice for
pregnancy and the post-natal period.

The Complete Home Guide to All the Vitamins by Ruth Adams
All you want to know about vitamins.

Why Aluminium Pans Are Dangerous by Edgar J. Saxon
Facts regarding the hazards of aluminum pans.

63 Meatless Meals by Bridget Amies
A practical selection of recipes to help you prepare balanced meals.

Children's Diet by Bircher-Benner
Bircher-Benner's principles of diet as applied to children.

Everybody's Guide to Nature Cure by Harry Benjamin
A complete guide to the principles of naturopathy.

Better Sight Without Glasses by Harry Benjamin
How to improve your sight with diet and exercise.

What's Cooking by Eva Batt
The vegan guide to good eating.

The Oxford Book of Food Plants by G. B. Masefield, M. Wallis, S. G.
Harrison & B. E. Nicholson
A colorfully illustrated book describing 420 different plants that serve
the human race for food.

Herbs for Health and Cookery by Claire Loewenfeld & Philippa Back
All about herbs and how to use them.

The Uses of Juices by C. E. Clinkard
Information regarding the inestimable value of freshly extracted raw fruit and vegetable juices and the purpose for which each juice is used.

A–Z of Health Foods by Carol Bowen
A handy A–Z glossary providing information on the use, preparation, cooking instructions and storage of health foods, together with a recipe section.

Healthy Eating for the New Age by Joyce d'Silva
Excellent and varied recipes that adhere to health foods as well as vegan principles.

Prescription for Energy by Charles De Coty Marsh
This book provides for sufferers from rheumatism and allied complaints precisely what it states–a prescription for energy. The author's researches over the years have enabled him to be specific on diets and menus.

The Complete Raw Juice Therapy by Susan E. Charmine
A most comprehensive guide to the healing and regenerative powers of natural energy from raw juices.

A Guide to the Bach Flower Remedies by Julian Barnard
A guide to the Bach remedies (discovered in the 1930s by Edward Bach), which are a simple and natural method of healing through the use of certain wild flowers, the remedies being used to treat the personality disorders of the patient rather than the individual physical condition.

Let's Cook It Right by Adelle Davis
A popular and helpful cookbook dedicated to the principle that foods can be prepared to retain both flavor and nutrients.

Diet for a Small Planet by Frances Moore Lappé
High protein meatless cooking with proper food combining.

Guide to color photographs

Soups

1. Country vegetable soup
2. Carrot potage
3. Cream of spinach & zucchini soup
4. Russian vegetable soup
5. Whole wheat rusks
6. Cheese scones

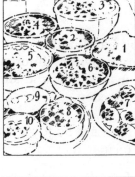

Salads

1. Endive & oranges with cheese dressing
2. Waldorf salad
3. Green Salad
4. Whole wheat mayonnaise
5. Hawaiian rice salad
6. Italian pasta salad
7. Eggs Indienne
8. Hummus
9. Cream cheese & cashew nut pâté
10. Mushroom pâté

Savouries

1. Jacket eggs
2. Nut loaf with cheese & tomato layer
3. Green salad
4. Eggplant & red bean stew
5. Nut Roast
6. Tomato & cheese pizza
7. Leek & cheese quiche
8. Homity pies
9. Spinach roll

Puddings & Desserts

1. Lemon meringue pie
2. Sticky prune cake
3. Orange & banana trifle
4. Lemon cheesecake
5. Sunshine pie
6. Creamy bran & apple chunks

Cakes & Biscuits

1. Millet & peanut cookies
2. Fruit scones
3. Raw sugar meringues
4. Iced carrot cake
5. Carob chip cookies
6. Coconut biscuits
7. Truffle triangle
8. Date & coconut gâteau
9. Drop scones
10. Barabrith
11. Honey buns
12. Honey cake

Breads

1. Barley bread
2. Cranks whole wheat bread
3. Whole wheat rolls
4. Cheese loaf
5. Bran loaf
6. Oatmeal soda bread
7. Chelsea buns
8. Spiced currant bread
9. Pumpernickel
10. Rye bread

Cranks Cheese Buns

These won an *Evening Standard* award for the best sandwich in London!

Juices

1. Carrot, orange & honey drink
2. Raspberry yogurt drink
3. Tiger's milk - a Gaylord Hauser recipe
4. Cranks home-made lemonade
5. Watercress, tomato & apple drink
6. Tomato juice
7. Curvacious cocktail - a Gaylord Hauser recipe
8. Cucumber, lemon & honey drink

SOUPS

Anyone who has been to France, particularly in the country areas, will have savored the taste of a home-made soup (potage) often made while you wait. It is satisfying to know that something is made with loving care, on the premises, and with fresh ingredients. Such are the soups made in all of the Cranks restaurants—never out of a can—and made from scratch every morning.

Home-made soups are truly delicious and very easy to make, so once you have tasted them you will never want to serve the canned variety again. Most vegetables, beans, and legumes and even some fruits and nuts may be used to make soup, either chopped in a broth to give a wholesome and hearty soup, or blended in a blender to make a puréed soup that can then be enriched with cream.

A blender is a very useful piece of equipment for producing puréed soups quickly and efficiently, but if you do not have one it is possible to achieve similar results by pressing the contents of the soup through a strainer or vegetable mill.

It is very important to remember that to make a really nourishing and well-flavored soup you need stock, so do save every drop of vegetable water that is left over when cooking vegetables, and keep it covered in the refrigerator to use as required. If vegetable water is not available, dissolve a vegetable stock cube in water as directed on the package, or in place of the stock use Bran water or Oatmeal water *(see recipe page 47)*. Some soups include milk as part of their liquid content, so for those following a non-dairy diet, soy milk *(see page 32)* should be used instead.

Soups are ideal for family eating, picnic, or packed lunches and dinner parties. For these special occasions presentation is important and can be improved by garnishing the soup with one of the following:

> chopped parsley or other fresh herbs
> grated cheese
> chopped nuts
> small pieces of sautéed vegetable to correspond with the flavor of the soup
> croûtons—small cubes of whole wheat bread, sautéed until crisp
> a swirl of yogurt or fresh cream

Bran water

This can be used as stock in soups and stews or as part of liquid content in bread.

Bran 2 cups
Water 3¾ cups

Makes about 3¾ cups

Mix bran and water together. Cover and let stand overnight. Strain, cover, and refrigerate. Use as required.

Oatmeal water

Use ¾ cup fine oatmeal in place of bran. Continue as recipe above.

Creamy onion soup

Medium-sized onions 2
Small potato 1
Butter or margarine 2 tbsp
Milk 2 cups
Vegetable stock 1 cup
Bay leaf 1
Salt & pepper to taste

Serves 4-6

Chop onion and potato. Melt butter and sauté onions until transparent. Add remaining ingredients, bring to a boil, reduce heat, and simmer, covered, 20 minutes. Remove bay leaf. Allow to cool slightly, then blend in small quantities in a blender. Reheat to serving temperature and adjust seasoning to taste.

Green pea soup

An economical and hearty soup, ideal for cold winter days.

Green split peas 1 cup
Water 5 cups
Large onion 1
Butter or margarine 4 tbsp
Vegetable stock cubes 2
Salt & pepper to taste

Serves 4-6

Wash peas well, then soak in measured water overnight. Chop onion. Melt butter in a saucepan and sauté onion until transparent. Add peas to water and stock cubes. Stir until stock cubes dissolve, then simmer 1 hour. Season to taste. If desired, blend in a blender.

Cream of watercress soup

A delicately flavored soup that can be served hot or chilled.

Medium-sized onion 1
Small potato 1
Butter or margarine 2 tbsp
Bunch watercress 1
Milk 1 cup
Vegetable stock 1 cup
Salt & pepper to taste
Fresh heavy cream ¼ cup

Serves 4

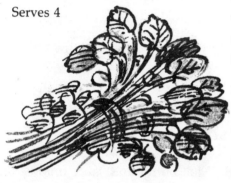

Chop onion and potato. Melt butter in a saucepan and sauté onion until transparent. Add potato, watercress, milk, and stock. Bring to a boil, reduce heat, cover, and simmer 20 minutes. Allow to cool slightly, then blend in small amounts in a blender. Return to pan, adjust seasoning to taste, stir in cream, and reheat to serving temperature.

To serve chilled
Chill before stirring in cream. Serve with a swirl of cream and a few sprigs of watercress to garnish.

Mangetout soup

Mangetout literally means "eat all" in French—sometimes called sugar peas.

Medium-sized onion 1
Mangetout (sugar peas or snow
 peas) 1 cup
Small potato 1
Butter or margarine 2 tbsp
Vegetable stock 2 cups
Milk 1 cup
Salt & pepper to taste

Serves 4-6

Top and tail, and then wash mangetout. Coarsely chop vegetables. Melt butter and sauté onion until transparent. Add mangetout, potato, and stock. Bring to a boil, reduce heat, cover, and simmer 20 minutes. Off the heat, stir in milk. Blend soup in a blender in small quantities. Return to pan, adjust seasoning to taste, and reheat to serving temperature.

To serve chilled
Chill before adding milk. Serve with a swirl of cream.

Borscht

Originally from Russia, this soup is dramatic in color and exciting in flavor. Serve hot or chilled.

Medium-sized onion 1
Small potato 1
Raw beets 1 lb
Butter or margarine 2 tbsp
Vegetable stock 5 cups
Cider vinegar 3 tbsp

Chop vegetables. Melt butter and sauté onion until transparent. Add potato, beets, and stock and bring to a boil. Reduce heat, cover, and simmer ½ hour. Allow to cool before blending in small amounts in a blender. Return to saucepan, add remaining

Vegex 1 tsp
Salt & pepper to taste
Ground nutmeg to taste
Sour cream or natural yogurt
   to garnish
Chopped parsley to garnish

Serves 6

ingredients, and season generously. Reheat to serving temperature. Stir in sour cream just before serving and sprinkle with chopped parsley.

To serve chilled
Blend soup and stir in remaining ingredients. Cover and chill until needed. Garnish as above.

Cream of leek soup

Large leeks 2
Small potato 1
Medium-sized carrot 1
Butter or margarine 2 tbsp
Vegetable stock 5 cups
Salt & pepper to taste
Heavy cream ½ cup

Serves 6

Chop vegetables. Melt butter and sauté vegetables a few minutes, stirring occasionally. Add stock, bring to a boil, reduce heat, cover, and simmer 20 minutes. Allow to cool slightly before blending in small amounts in a blender. Return to saucepan and adjust seasoning to taste. Stir in cream and reheat to serving temperature without boiling.

To serve chilled
Chill after blending and stir in cream just before serving.

Cream of spinach & zucchini soup

One of the most popular and sophisticated soups at Cranks, this is ideal for special occasions.

Medium-sized onion 1
Large zucchini 1
Medium-sized potato 1
Spinach 1 cup
Oil 2 tbsp
Few sprigs parsley
Vegetable stock 5 cups
Heavy cream ½ cup
Salt & pepper to taste

Serves 4-6

Chop vegetables. Heat oil in a saucepan and sauté onion and zucchini until onion is transparent. Add potato, spinach, parsley, and stock. Bring to a boil, reduce heat, cover, and simmer 20 minutes. Allow to cool before blending in small quantities in a blender. Return soup to saucepan, stir in cream, and adjust seasoning to taste. Reheat gently without boiling. If wished, garnish with a swirl of heavy cream.

Fresh tomato soup

Delicate in color with an exciting flavor, this soup bears no resemblance to the canned varieties.

Medium-sized onion 1
Small potato 1
Tomatoes 1 lb
Butter or margarine 4 tbsp
Garlic cloves 2
Bay leaf 1
Tomato paste 2 tbsp
Vegetable stock 2 cups
Milk 2 cups
Salt & pepper to taste

Serves 4-6

Chop onion and potato. Quarter tomatoes. Melt butter and sauté onion until transparent. Add potato, tomatoes, garlic, bay leaf, tomato paste, and stock. Cover and simmer 20 minutes. Off the heat, stir in milk. Remove bay leaf. Blend in small quantities in a blender. Adjust seasoning to taste and reheat to serving temperature.

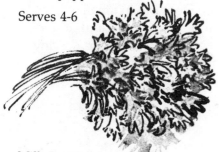

Apple & peanut butter soup

An unusual combination of ingredients gives this soup an original and exciting flavor.

Milk 5 cups
Medium-sized cooking apple 1
Peanut butter 4 tbsp
Lemon, juice of 1
Oatmeal 3 tbsp
Ground ginger ¼ tsp
Salt & pepper to taste
Chopped parsley to garnish

Serves 6

Heat milk to just below boiling point. Grate apple. Blend together peanut butter and lemon juice, and add to milk with remaining ingredients. Simmer 15 minutes. Allow to cool slightly, then blend in small quantities in a blender. Reheat to serving temperature and adjust seasoning to taste. Sprinkle with chopped parsley.

This soup may be served chilled if wished.

Mushroom soup

A true favorite!

Medium-sized onion 1
Small potato 1
Mushrooms 2 to 3 cups
Butter or margarine 4 tbsp
Thyme 1 tsp
Large sprig parsley
Milk 3 cups
Salt & pepper to taste

Serves 4-6

Chop vegetables. Melt butter in a saucepan and sauté onion until transparent. Add potato and mushrooms and cook, stirring, 2 minutes. Add remaining ingredients, bring to a boil, reduce heat, cover, and simmer 20 minutes. Allow to cool slightly, then blend in a blender until smooth. Reheat to serving temperature, and adjust seasoning to taste.

Mulligatawny soup

A spicy, nourishing soup.

Medium-sized carrot 1
Medium-sized onion 1
Medium-sized potato 1
Medium-sized cooking apple 1
Oil 2 tbsp
Garlic cloves, crushed 2
Curry powder 1 tbsp
Tomato juice 1 cup
Vegetable stock 5 cups
Salt to taste

Serves 6

Chop vegetables and apple. Heat oil in a large saucepan and sauté vegetables and apple until onion is transparent. Add garlic and curry powder and cook, stirring, 2 minutes. Add all the liquids, bring to a boil, reduce heat, cover, and simmer 30 minutes. Allow to cool slightly, then blend in small quantities in a blender. Reheat to serving temperature and adjust seasoning to taste.

Creamy potato soup

Medium-sized potatoes 2
Medium-sized onion 1
Oil 2 tbsp
Vegetable stock 2 cups
Milk 1 cup
Mixed herbs 1 tsp
Paprika 1 tsp
Caraway seeds ½ tsp
Salt & pepper to taste

Serves 4-6

Chop vegetables. Heat oil in a saucepan and sauté vegetables until onion is transparent, then add remaining ingredients. Bring to a boil, reduce heat, cover, and simmer 20 minutes. Blend soup in a blender in small quantities. Thin with a little extra milk if desired. Adjust seasoning to taste and reheat to serving temperature.

Carrot potage

This is based on a traditional French recipe.

Carrots 1 lb
Medium-sized potato 1
Medium-sized onion 1
Butter or margarine 2 tbsp
Thyme & sage 1 tsp each
Vegetable stock 5 cups
Vegex 1 tsp
Salt & pepper to taste

Serves 4-6

Chop vegetables. Melt butter, add onion, and sauté until transparent. Add remaining ingredients, bring to a boil, reduce heat, and simmer, covered, ½ hour. Allow to cool slightly, then blend in small quantities in a blender until smooth. Reheat to serving temperature, and adjust seasoning to taste.

Buckwheat & potato soup

A nourishing soup with a distinctive flavor.

Medium-sized potato 1
Medium-sized onion 1
Vegetable stock 3¾ cups
Buckwheat ⅔ cup
Parsley, chopped 2 tbsp
Oregano ½ tsp
Vegex 1 tsp
Milk 2¼ cups
Soy sauce 1 tsp
Salt & pepper to taste

Serves 4-6

Chop potato and onion. Bring stock to a boil in a saucepan, then add buckwheat, vegetables, parsley, oregano, and Vegex. Simmer, covered, about ½ hour, until buckwheat and vegetables are tender. After 15 minutes, check to see if cooking liquid has been absorbed. If necessary, stir in half the milk. Allow to cool slightly, then blend in a blender in small quantities, adding remaining milk as required. Add soy sauce and seasoning, then reheat to serving temperature. Adjust seasoning to taste. Thin with extra milk or stock as necessary. If wished, top with grated cheese to serve.

Carrot, apple & cashew nut soup

Carrots 1 lb
Large onion 1
Small potato 1
Large cooking apple 1
Butter or margarine 4 tbsp
Vegetable stock 5 cups
Broken cashew nuts ½ cup
Salt & pepper to taste

Serves 6

Coarsely chop vegetables and apple. Melt butter in a large saucepan and sauté prepared vegetables 5 minutes, stirring occasionally. Add remaining ingredients, bring to a boil, cover, and simmer 30 minutes until vegetables are just tender. Allow to cool before blending in a blender. Reheat to serving temperature, and adjust seasoning to taste.

Armenian soup

A Marshall Street restaurant favorite, this recipe was introduced by a member of the staff many years ago.

Red lentils, washed ⅓ cup
Dried apricots, washed ½ cup
Large potato 1
Vegetable stock 5 cups
Lemon, juice of ½
Ground cumin 1 tsp
Parsley, chopped 3 tbsp
Salt & pepper to taste

Serves 4-6

Place lentils and apricots in a large saucepan. Coarsely chop potato and add to pan with remaining ingredients. Bring to a boil, cover, and simmer 30 minutes. Allow to cool, then blend in a blender until smooth. Reheat to serving temperature, and adjust seasoning to taste.

Egg & lemon soup

Medium-sized carrots 2 to 3
Medium-sized onion 1
Butter or margarine 2 tbsp
Vegetable stock 2 cups
Lemon 1
Bay leaf (or ground bay leaf) 1
Milk 1 cup
Organic eggs 2
Salt & pepper to taste

Serves 4-6

Chop vegetables. Melt butter in a large saucepan and sauté vegetables until onion is transparent. Add stock, grated rind from lemon, and bay leaf. Bring to a boil, reduce heat, cover, and simmer 25 minutes, then remove bay leaf. Off the heat, stir in the milk, blend in a blender in small quantities, then return to saucepan. Squeeze juice from lemon. Beat eggs and lemon juice together and whisk them into soup. Reheat very carefully to serving temperature. *Do not allow to boil.* Adjust seasoning to taste.

Cheddar cheese soup

Medium-sized onion 1
Medium-sized potato 1
Large carrot 1
Butter or margarine 2 tbsp
Vegetable stock 2 cups
Garlic clove, crushed 1
Thyme & sage ½ tsp each
Milk 1 cup
Cheddar cheese, grated 1½ cups
Salt & pepper to taste

Serves 4-6

Chop vegetables. Melt butter in a large saucepan and sauté vegetables until onion is transparent. Add stock, garlic, and herbs. Bring to a boil, reduce heat, cover, and simmer 25 minutes. Add remaining ingredients, allow to cool slightly, then blend in a blender in small quantities until smooth. Reheat very carefully to serving temperature. Do not allow to boil or the cheese will become stringy. Adjust seasoning to taste.

Celery & cashew nut soup

Medium-sized onion 1
Medium-sized potato 1
Celery ½ head
Butter or margarine 2 tbsp
Broken cashew nuts ⅔ cup
Vegetable stock 3 cups
Milk 2 cups
Salt & pepper to taste

Serves 4-6

Chop vegetables. Melt butter in a large saucepan and sauté prepared vegetables gently until onion is transparent. Add cashews and continue cooking 5 minutes, stirring frequently. Add stock, bring to a boil, cover, and simmer 20 minutes. Add milk, allow to cool slightly, then blend in a blender in small quantities. Reheat to serving temperature, and adjust seasoning to taste.

Parsnip & apple soup

An unusual combination of vegetable and fruit gives this soup an exciting flavor.

Butter or margarine 2 tbsp
Medium-sized onion 1
Medium-sized parsnips 2
Medium-sized cooking apple 1
Vegetable stock 2¼ cups
Parsley, chopped 2 tbsp
Mixed herbs ½ tsp
Milk 2¼ cups
Salt & pepper to taste

Serves 4-6

Chop vegetables. Melt butter in a large saucepan and sauté vegetables and apple, stirring frequently, until onion is transparent. Add stock and herbs, then bring to a boil and reduce heat. Cover and simmer 30 minutes. Add milk. Allow to cool slightly before blending in a blender in small quantities. Reheat to serving temperature, and adjust seasoning to taste.

Cauliflower soup

A deliciously delicate flavor makes this a soup to impress guests!

Medium-sized potato 1
Medium-sized onion 1
Medium-sized cauliflower 1
Butter or margarine 2 tbsp
Vegetable stock 2¼ cups
Parsley, chopped 2 tbsp
Ground nutmeg to taste
Milk 2¼ cups
Salt & pepper to taste

Serves 4-6

Chop potato and onion. Melt butter in a large saucepan and sauté vegetables until onion is transparent. Break cauliflower into florets and add to pan with stock, parsley, and nutmeg. Bring to a boil, reduce heat, cover, and simmer 20 minutes. Add milk and allow to cool before blending in a blender in small quantities. Reheat to serving temperature, adjust seasoning to taste, and serve at once.

Potage Malakoff

First introduced in Marshall Street, this is now a great favorite in all Cranks restaurants.

Medium-sized onion 1
Medium-sized potato 1
Large carrot 1
Large tomatoes 2
Butter or margarine 2 tbsp
Few sprigs parsley
Garlic clove, crushed 1
Bay leaf 1
Vegetable stock 5 cups
Soy sauce 2 tsp
Vegex 1 tsp
Salt & pepper to taste
Spinach, finely shredded 1 cup

Serves 4-6

Chop vegetables. Melt butter in a saucepan and sauté onion until transparent. Add remaining ingredients, except spinach. Bring to a boil, reduce heat, cover, and simmer 30 minutes. Allow to cool before blending in small amounts in a blender. Return to saucepan, add spinach, and simmer 10 minutes. Adjust seasoning to taste.

Russian vegetable soup

Medium-sized onion 1
Medium-sized potato 1
Medium-sized parsnip 1
Large carrot 1
Butter or margarine 4 tbsp
Parsley, chopped 2 tbsp
Mixed herbs ½ tsp
Nutmeg to taste
Vegetable stock 5 cups
Small leek 1
Cabbage, shredded ½ cup
Salt & pepper to taste

Serves 4-6

Chop onion, potato, parsnip, and carrots. Melt half the butter in a large saucepan and sauté vegetables gently, stirring occasionally, until onion is transparent. Add parsley, herbs, nutmeg, and stock and bring to a boil, reduce heat, cover, and simmer 30 minutes. Let cool before blending in a blender in small quantities. Meanwhile, finely shred leek and cabbage and sauté in remaining butter until just tender. Add to blended soup, simmer gently 10 minutes, and adjust seasoning to taste.

Pumpkin & spinach soup

An obvious choice for Halloween, but keep this recipe in mind during the short pumpkin season.

Medium-sized onion 1
Butter or margarine 2 tbsp
Pumpkin 1 lb
Spinach 2 cups
Medium-sized tomatoes 2
Vegetable stock 7½ cups
Salt & pepper to taste

Serves 6

Finely chop onion. Melt butter in a large saucepan and sauté onion until transparent. Dice pumpkin, finely shred spinach, and coarsely chop tomatoes. Add vegetables to pan with remaining ingredients. Bring to a boil, reduce heat, then cover and simmer about 20 minutes until all the vegetables are tender. Adjust seasoning to taste.

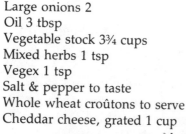

French onion soup

One of the great classic soups of all time. It makes a hearty meal served with whole wheat croûtons and grated cheese floating on the top.

Large onions 2
Oil 3 tbsp
Vegetable stock 3¾ cups
Mixed herbs 1 tsp
Vegex 1 tsp
Salt & pepper to taste
Whole wheat croûtons to serve
Cheddar cheese, grated 1 cup

Serves 4

Finely slice onions. Heat oil in a saucepan and sauté onions until golden brown. Add remaining ingredients and bring to a boil. Reduce heat, cover, and simmer 15 minutes. Serve with whole wheat croûtons and grated cheese.

Country vegetable soup

Medium-sized onion 1
Medium-sized potato 1
Small pepper 1
Medium-sized leek 1
Large zucchini 1
Oil 3 tbsp
Vegetable stock 5 cups
Tomato juice 2¼ cups
Garlic cloves, crushed 2
Bay leaf 1
Mixed herbs 1 tsp
Salt & pepper to taste

Serves 6

Chop onion, dice potato, cut pepper into thin strips, shred leek, slice zucchini. Heat oil in a large saucepan and sauté onion until transparent. Add remaining vegetables and sauté, stirring occasionally, 5 minutes. Add remaining ingredients and bring to a boil. Reduce heat, cover, and simmer about 30 minutes. Remove bay leaf. Adjust seasoning to taste.

Lentil & tomato soup

A hearty and satisfying soup. Sprinkle with grated cheese and this is a meal in itself!

Small onion 1
Medium-sized tomatoes 1 to 2
Oil 2 tbsp
Lentils ½ cup
Tomato juice 1 cup
Vegetable stock 3¾ cups
Thyme ½ tsp
Vegex ½ tsp
Salt & pepper to taste

Serves 4-6

Chop onion and tomatoes. Heat oil in a saucepan and sauté onion until transparent. Add remaining ingredients, cover, and simmer 30 minutes. Adjust seasoning to taste.

Chunky bean soup

Mixed dried beans 1 cup
Large onion 1
Medium-sized carrot 1
Butter or margarine 2 tbsp
Water 3¾ cups
Garlic cloves, crushed 2
Vegetable stock cubes 2
Tomato paste 2 tbsp
Vegex 1 tsp
Salt & pepper to taste
Chopped parsley to garnish

Serves 4-6

Wash beans well and soak in water overnight. Chop onion. Dice carrot. Melt butter and sauté onion until transparent. Put drained beans into measured water with remaining ingredients, except parsley. Simmer 1 hour, or until beans are tender. Adjust seasoning to taste. Sprinkle with parsley.

Hauser soup

This beautiful orange-colored soup was created by Gaylord Hauser, the American nutritionist, and appears in his book Look Younger, Live Longer—*a book that was a great inspiration to the directors in the setting-up of Cranks.*

Large carrots 2
Small onion 1
Milk 4 cups
Grated nutmeg to taste
Salt & pepper to taste
Chopped parsley to garnish

Serves 6

Coarsely chop vegetables. Place all ingredients, except parsley, in a blender and blend until smooth. Pour into a saucepan and heat slowly to just below boiling point. Adjust seasoning to taste. Serve at once, sprinkled with chopped parsley.

This can also be served as an iced soup, made ahead and refrigerated for several hours. Place in a blender and blend for a few seconds, then serve sprinkled with chopped parsley.

Gazpacho

A delicious cold soup based on an original recipe from Andalusia.

Cucumber ¼
Small green or red pepper 1
Medium-sized tomatoes 1 to 2
Small onion 1
Garlic clove 1
Few sprigs parsley
Tomato juice 1 cup
Water ½ cup
Tomato paste 1 tbsp
Salt & pepper to taste

Serves 4-6

Coarsely chop all the vegetables. Blend all ingredients together in small quantities in a blender until smooth. Chill and serve with croûtons.

STARTERS

Where does a "starter" finish and a "main course" start? The answer must be dependent on the viewpoint or mood of the cook. For in vegetarian cooking in particular a recipe used on one occasion as a main dish can, with very minor modifications and in smaller quantities, be a starter for another meal.

A vegetarian whole food regime tends to presuppose a simple mode of living, where the idea of a starter is out of place as too sophisticated. But there must be occasions when having friends to a meal spurs one on to attempt extra gastronomic delights, and a starter gives a chance to paint from a broader palette. Also, of course, on such occasions it can be helpful to give one's guests something to get on with and for conversation to develop while completing the preparations for the main course.

As an alternative to the usual half a grapefruit, avocado, salad, or soup, this chapter introduces you to some new recipe ideas including pâtés made with vegetables, cheese, and even yeast, as well as hot and cold vegetable dishes and egg recipes.

Tamari cashews

These delicious roasted nuts make compulsive eating. Serve them with drinks or as a protein snack at any time.

Oil 1 tbsp
Broken cashew nuts 2⅓ cups
Soy sauce 2 tbsp

Pour oil into a baking tin, add nuts and turn in oil. Roast at 350°F about 15 minutes, turning occasionally, until golden. Sprinkle soy sauce over and stir nuts until well coated. Return to oven 5 minutes. Stir again and let cool in the pan. Store in an airtight container.

Hummus

A tangy dip popular in Greek and Turkish restaurants. Make it at home and you can vary the flavor of lemon and garlic to suit your taste.

Chickpeas, soaked overnight
  1 cup
Water
Garlic clove 2
Oil 3 tbsp
Lemons, juice of 1-2
Natural yogurt 4 tbsp
Salt & pepper to taste
Chopped parsley to garnish
Paprika to garnish

Serves 6

Place chickpeas in a saucepan, and just cover with water. Add garlic cloves. Bring to a boil, cover, and simmer 30 minutes, adding extra water if necessary. Allow to cool in the water. Put oil, juice of 1 lemon, and yogurt into a blender, add half the chickpeas with cooking liquid and garlic, and blend until smooth. Keep adding chickpeas and extra water if necessary, until they have all been incorporated. Season with salt and pepper, adding extra lemon juice if wished. Transfer to a serving dish, sprinkle with chopped parsley and paprika, and serve with whole wheat bread or melba toast.

Garlic relish

The Cranks variation of a translated French recipe.

Whole wheat breadcrumbs ½ cup
Hot water ½ cup
Large onion 1
Butter or margarine 4 tbsp
Dried yeast 1½ tsp
Garlic cloves, crushed 2 to 3
Thyme 1 tbsp
Salt & pepper to taste

Serves 6

Soak breadcrumbs in hot water. Finely chop onion. Melt butter in a saucepan and sauté onion until transparent. Add soaked bread and any excess liquid and cook over high heat, stirring all the time until no excess liquid remains. Off heat, add yeast and remaining ingredients. Adjust seasoning. Beat well and press into a shallow serving dish. Cover and let

cool. Serve on individual plates with a green garnish and triangles of whole wheat toast.

This can also be used as a spread or sandwich filling.

Mushroom pâté

A variation of Garlic relish and equally as good.

Medium-sized onion 1
Mushrooms 1 lb
Butter or margarine 4 tbsp
Whole wheat breadcrumbs
1½ cups
Hot water ½ cup
Lemon, juice of ½
Garlic cloves, crushed (optional)
    1-2
Dried yeast, 1 tbsp
Ground nutmeg to taste
Salt & pepper to taste

Serves 6

Finely chop onion, mushroom caps, and stalks. Melt butter in a saucepan and sauté onion until transparent. Add mushrooms and cook a further 2-3 minutes. Soak breadcrumbs in hot water, then add to mushrooms with lemon juice and garlic. Cook over gentle heat until no excess liquid remains. Off heat, beat in remaining ingredients and check seasoning. Spoon into a serving dish, cover, and refrigerate until needed. Garnish with raw mushroom slices.

This can also be used as a spread or sandwich filling.

Cream cheese & cashew nut pâté

Small carrot 1
Cream cheese 1 cup
Broken cashew nuts, roasted &
    ground ¾ cup
Chopped parsley 1 tbsp
Salt & pepper to taste
Parsley to garnish

Serves 4-6

Finely grate carrot. Beat all the ingredients together in a bowl. Press mixture into individual dishes, cover, and refrigerate until needed. Garnish with parsley sprigs and slices of raw carrot. Serve with toast.

This can also be used as a spread or sandwich filling.

Wine & nut pâté

This pâté was first introduced into our "Dine & Wine" evenings. It's a very special recipe and needs weighing out accurately. Ideal for entertaining, as it can be made a day or two before it is needed.

Onion, small 1
Celery sticks 2
Butter or margarine 1 tbsp
Ground cumin 1 tsp

Grease and line the base of a 5 x 9 inch loaf pan. Peel and finely chop onion. Trim and finely chop celery. Melt butter in a saucepan and sauté vegetables until soft. Add spices and herbs and cook, stirring, 1 minute.

Paprika 1 tsp
Basil 1 tsp
Vegetable stock or water ½ cup
Red wine ½ cup
*Cooked chestnuts, ground
    ½ cup
Shelled walnuts, ground ¾ cup
Shelled pecans, ground ¾ cup
Whole wheat breadcrumbs ½ cup
Chopped parsley 4 tbsp
Garlic clove, crushed 1
Soy sauce 1 tbsp
Brandy 1 tbsp
Organic eggs 2
Salt & pepper to taste

Serves 6-8

Add vegetable stock and wine and bring to a boil. Off the heat, stir in nuts, breadcrumbs, parsley, garlic, soy sauce, and brandy. Mix well, then add beaten eggs and season generously.

Spoon mixture into prepared pan and level surface. Bake at 350°F about 40 minutes, or until slightly firm to the touch. Leave to go cold in pan, then turn out on a plate. Serve in slices.

For a decorative finish make up ½ cup agar-agar following the instructions on the package. Brush top and sides of pâté with agar-agar and arrange lemon slices along its length. Brush a second time with agar-agar to glaze loaf completely.

*Use fresh chestnuts where possible. Make a slash in 1 cup chestnuts to pierce skins. Bring to a boil in water, cover, and simmer 30 minutes. Cool and remove skins. Alternatively, use ½ cup canned chestnuts.

Egg & tomato mousse

Organic eggs, hard-boiled &
    shelled 6
Medium-sized tomatoes 2
Small green pepper ½
Milk 2 tbsp
Mayonnaise *(see page 87)*
    3 tbsp
Salt & pepper to taste
Agar-agar 2 tsp
Water ½ cup
Tomato slices to garnish

Serves 6

Coarsely chop eggs, quarter tomatoes, and chop pepper. Place in a blender with milk and mayonnaise. Blend until smooth. Season generously. Dissolve agar-agar in water according to instructions on label. Off the heat, beat some of the egg mixture into agar-agar, then return this mixture to the bulk. Stir well to mix evenly, then spoon into a serving dish or individual dishes. Cover and refrigerate until needed. Garnish with tomato slices. Serve with toast.

Baked grapefruit–I

This is good at breakfast or as a dessert.

Grapefruit 2
Honey 4 tsp
Ground cinnamon

Serves 4

Cut grapefruit in half. Remove central pith with a grapefruit knife, then loosen segments. Pour honey into center of each grapefruit half and sprinkle with cinnamon, if wished. Bake at 375°F about 15 minutes. Serve warm.

Baked grapefruit–II

Grapefruit 2
Raw sugar 4 tsp
Butter or margarine 2 tbsp
Ground cinnamon 1 tsp

Serves 4

Cut grapefruit in half. Remove central pith with a grapefruit knife, then loosen segments. Mix together sugar, butter, and cinnamon and spread over fruit. Bake at 375°F about 15 minutes. Serve warm.

Florida salad

This is also ideal for breakfast or as a dessert.

Medium-sized grapefruit 2
Medium-sized oranges 2
Honey 2 tbsp

Serves 4

Peel grapefruit and oranges, removing all white membrane. Using a sharp knife free fruit segments from membrane. Squeeze out any excess juice and reserve. Arrange segments in a serving dish. Mix honey and fruit juice together and pour over fruit. Cover and leave in a cool place to marinate.

Mushrooms à la grecque

Water ½ cup
Garlic cloves, finely chopped 2
Lemons, juice of 2
Olive oil 2 tbsp
Salt & pepper to taste
Bay leaf 1
Sprig of parsley 1
Button mushrooms 3 to 4 cups
Large tomato 1
Chopped parsley to garnish

Serves 4-6

Put the first 7 ingredients into a saucepan. Bring to a boil and boil 5 minutes. Add mushrooms and simmer, covered, a further 5 minutes. Add chopped tomato, then refrigerate until really cold. Sprinkle with chopped parsley before serving.

This can also be served as a salad.

Ratatouille

This speciality from Provence is good served hot or cold.

Medium-sized onion 1
Large red or green pepper 1
Large eggplant 1
Large zucchini 2
Oil 4 tbsp
Tomatoes 6
Garlic cloves, crushed 2-3
Oregano ½ tsp
Basil ½ tsp
Tomato juice 2 cups
Salt & pepper to taste

Serves 4-6

Chop onion and pepper, dice eggplant, and slice zucchini. Heat oil in a large saucepan, add onion and eggplant and sauté until onion is transparent. Add zucchini and pepper and sauté a further 5 minutes, stirring occasionally. Add remaining ingredients and simmer, covered, 15-20 minutes. Serve hot or cold.

Stuffed tomatoes

A summer special suitable for picnics and parties.

Medium-sized firm tomatoes 6
Fresh whole wheat breadcrumbs
    2 cups
Cream cheese ½ cup
Scallions or chives, chopped
    2 tbsp
Salt & pepper to taste
Parsley sprigs to garnish

Makes 6

Wash and dry tomatoes. Cut a lid off the top of each and scoop out and chop pulp. Leave tomato shells upside down on paper towels to drain. Add breadcrumbs, cream cheese, and onion to tomato pulp and beat well. Season to taste. Fill tomatoes with cheese mixture, replace lids, and garnish each with a sprig of parsley. Refrigerate until needed.

Creamy baked tomatoes

Very large tomatoes 4
Salt & pepper to taste
Basil 1 tsp
Heavy cream 4 tbsp
Cheddar cheese, grated ½ cup
    or Parmesan, grated ¼ cup

Serves 4

Halve tomatoes and place in individual ovenproof dishes. Sprinkle generously with salt, pepper, and basil. Bake at 400°F 10 minutes. Spoon cream over and sprinkle with cheese. Return to oven for a further 10 minutes. Serve at once.

Tarragon eggs en cocotte

To make a tasty main meal, double the quantity of ingredients and bake in one large, shallow, ovenproof dish.

Small onion 1
Medium-sized tomatoes 1 to 2
Butter or margarine 2 tbsp
Tarragon 1 tsp
Salt & pepper to taste
Organic eggs 4
Heavy cream 4 tbsp

Serves 4

Finely chop onion and tomatoes. Melt butter in a saucepan and sauté onion until transparent. Add tomatoes and tarragon and cook over low heat, stirring frequently until soft and pulpy. Adjust seasoning to taste. Spoon mixture into 4 individual ovenproof dishes. Make a well in the center and break an egg into each one. Spoon cream over and bake at 400°F 10-15 minutes, or until done. Serve at once.

Eggs Indienne

An interesting variation of stuffed eggs—good for party food.

Small onion 1
Large tomato 1
Butter or margarine 2 tbsp
Curry powder 1 tsp
Golden seedless raisins 1 tbsp
Lemon juice to taste
Salt to taste
Organic eggs, hard-boiled &
  shelled 6
Sprigs of parsley to garnish

Serves 4-6

Finely chop onion and tomato. Melt butter in a saucepan and sauté onion until transparent. Stir in curry powder and cook 1-2 minutes. Add tomato, golden raisins, and a squeeze of lemon juice and cook, stirring, until soft and pulpy. Allow to cool. Cut eggs in half lengthwise, scoop out yolks, and rub through a sieve. Mix yolks with curry mixture, then spoon into halved eggs. Garnish with sprigs of parsley.

Egg mayonnaise

Small lettuce, finely shredded 1
Organic eggs, hard-boiled &
  shelled 4
Mayonnaise *(see page 87)* ½ cup
Paprika to garnish

Serves 4

Arrange a bed of shredded lettuce on 1 large or 4 individual plates. Cut eggs in half lengthwise and arrange cut-side down on lettuce. Coat with mayonnaise (thinned with a little milk, if necessary) and sprinkle with paprika.

Nut "cheese" *(vegan)*

Cranks own version of a vegan substitute for dairy cheese.

Margarine 8 tbsp
Mixed nuts, finely ground
   1⅓ cups
Vegex 1 tsp

Serves 4-6

Melt margarine over gentle heat. Stir in ground nuts and Vegex. Pour "cheese" into a container, cover, and refrigerate until set. Serve with whole wheat toast.

Sava *(vegan)*

A soy-based alternative to dairy cheese. Try the variations listed below, then experiment with other flavors.

Margarine 8 tbsp
Soy flour 1 cup
Garlic clove, crushed 1
Vegex 1 tsp

Serves 4

Melt margarine in a saucepan over low heat. Stir in soy flour and cook, stirring, a few minutes, or until slightly thickened. Off the heat, stir in garlic and yeast extract. Pour into a container, cover, and chill until set.

VARIATIONS
Curry Stir in 1 tsp curry powder with soy flour.

Tomato Stir in 1-2 tbsp tomato paste. Omit garlic.

Herb Add freshly chopped herbs to taste.

Soy curd "cheese" *(vegan)*

A soy-based alternative to dairy cheese made by the traditional method.

Soy flour 1 cup
Water 2¼ cups
Lemons, juice of 2
Salt & pepper to taste

Serves 4-6

Mix soy flour to a paste with some of the water. Bring remaining water to a boil, pour on soy paste, then return to saucepan. Bring to a boil, stirring continuously, then simmer 5 minutes. Off the heat, stir in lemon juice and let cool. Place some dampened cheesecloth in a large sieve over a bowl. Pour contents of saucepan on to cheesecloth and leave until all the liquid has drained through, producing a firm curd. Adjust seasoning to taste. For added flavor, stir in chopped herbs or crushed garlic.

SALADS

Salads are as good, or as bad, as their basic ingredients, so it is always important to start with good quality vegetables and fruit. How often one has seen limp lettuce leaves arranged on a plate with a few slices of cucumber and tomato and been told that it is a salad. A salad should be a delightful combination of flavors, color, and texture. This is achieved by carefully considering the ingredients and producing a well-balanced mixture. For example, crisp beansprouts combine extremely well with the soft, sweet texture of sliced banana and the richness of roasted peanuts; when tossed in a slightly spicy ginger dressing, they make a perfect salad.

Cranks produces a selection of salads every morning, which are sold in the restaurants and as take-out food. The combination of ingredients will vary with the seasons. In winter raw, grated root vegetables, cooked or sprouted beans, and rice or pasta are among the most popular bases. In summer there is a wealth of choice among the more delicate leaf vegetables and typical salad ingredients.

The combination of ingredients is almost limitless when it comes to making salad, as most vegetables and fruits combine well and complement each other. Nuts, seeds, dried fruit, and herbs can all add extra flavor and texture. It is also true that too many ingredients can spoil a salad mixture; it is necessary to be able to taste the individual ingredients that go into the salad.

If you are making a selection of salads at home, always start with a variety of basic ingredients. For example, potato, shredded red cabbage, green leaves, and a fruit such as apple or orange would constitute a good cross-section, in terms of color and texture. Preparation of the ingredients is important. A lot of the goodness in fruit and vegetables lies in or just below the skin, so wash, scrub, and trim them as necessary, but never peel unless absolutely essential. This is a general principle in the preparation of all fruit and vegetables and cannot be over-emphasized.

Having prepared the salad, the next stage is to dress it. This involves tossing the salad in a dressing, which may be a thick, creamy one, such as mayonnaise, or a thinner one such as French dressing. Whichever you choose, it is important to coat the salad ingredients well with the dressing but not to swamp the salad in too much liquid.

TO TOSS A SALAD

A tossed salad should be one in which the ingredients are just coated with dressing so that they glisten. There should not be an excess of dressing in the bottom of the salad bowl. To do this, place the salad in a large bowl, pour a little dressing over the salad, and using salad servers or two spoons, carefully turn the salad ingredients in a rotating movement until evenly coated. Add a little more dressing if necessary and repeat.

As a general rule, green leaf salads should be tossed just before serving. Root vegetable salads, marinated salads, and those tossed in mayonnaise will improve if dressed the day before, and will keep in a refrigerator for two or three days. The exceptions to this include watery vegetables, particularly tomatoes, which lose their flavor if kept for more than 24 hours.

Carrot mayonnaise

A colorful salad that may be kept for a few days in the refrigerator.

Carrots 1 lb
Mayonnaise *(see page 87)*
  ½ cup
Sunflower seeds ¼ cup
Chopped parsley 4 tbsp
Salt & pepper to taste

Serves 4-6

Finely grate carrots, stir in mayonnaise, sunflower seeds, and parsley. Season to taste. Cover and chill until needed.

Coleslaw

Coleslaw is cabbage salad, but it is far more interesting than its name suggests. This is the most popular combination of ingredients, but experiment with others to make new variations.

Small white cabbage 1
Medium-sized carrots 2
Small onion 1
Mayonnaise *(see page 87)*
  1 cup
Caraway seeds ½ tsp

Serves 6

Shred cabbage, grate carrot, and finely chop onion. Combine all ingredients in a mixing bowl. Toss well. Cover and chill until needed.

This will keep for several days in a refrigerator.

Cucumber in tarragon dressing

The delicate flavors of cucumber and tarragon complement each other very successfully to make this a refreshing salad.

French dressing *(see page 87)*
    4 tbsp
Tarragon, chopped ½ tsp
Cucumber 1
Salt & pepper to taste

Serves 4-6

Combine dressing and tarragon in a mixing bowl. Score the length of the cucumber with a fork. Dice cucumber and toss in dressing. Adjust seasoning to taste. Cover and chill until needed.

This will keep for 2-3 days in a refrigerator.

Waldorf salad

This is a winner at the latest Cranks branch in Covent Garden Market.

Celery sticks 4
Walnuts ½ cup
Large dessert apple 1
Cheddar cheese 1 cup
Mayonnaise *(see page 87)*
    ½ cup
Salt & pepper to taste

Serves 4-6

Chop celery and walnuts. Dice apple and cheese. Mix all the ingredients together in a salad bowl. Adjust seasoning to taste.

Spinach & mushroom salad

Whole wheat bread 4 slices
Garlic cloves, chopped 2
Oil ½ cup
Fresh spinach 2 cups

Cut bread into ½" cubes. Heat garlic and oil together in a frying pan. Remove garlic when it has browned, and sauté bread cubes until crisp and golden. Drain on paper towels and leave until cold. Shred spinach

Button mushrooms 1 cup
French dressing *(see page 87)*
    6 tbsp
Lemon, grated rind of ½
Salt & pepper to taste

Serves 4-6

into small pieces and slice mushrooms. Put spinach, mushrooms, and croûtons in a salad bowl. Mix dressing and lemon rind and toss salad. Adjust seasoning and serve at once.

Beet, celery & orange salad

Raw beets 1 cup
Celery sticks, trimmed 2
Small orange, grated rind &
    juice of 1
French dressing *(see page 87)*
    3 tbsp
Garlic clove, crushed 1

Serves 4-6

Grate beets and chop celery. Put beets and celery in a salad bowl. Combine orange rind and juice, French dressing, and garlic. Pour over vegetables and toss well. Cover and chill until needed.

This will keep for 2-3 days in a refrigerator.

Potato salad

Potatoes 2 lb
Small onion 1
French dressing *(see page 87)*
    ½ cup
Chopped parsley 4 tbsp
Salt & pepper to taste

Serves 6

Cut up potatoes (if using small new potatoes, leave whole) and steam for about 20 minutes, or until just tender, then dice. Finely chop onion. Place potatoes and onion in a bowl and pour over dressing while still warm. Toss well. Cover and chill until needed. Stir in parsley before serving, and adjust seasoning to taste.

This will keep for several days in a refrigerator.

Carrot & rutabaga in sour cream dressing

Raw carrots are always popular in salads, but this unusual combination of raw vegetables is surprisingly good.

Rutabaga 1½ cups
Medium-sized carrots 2 to 3
Sour cream dressing *(see page 87)*
    1 recipe

Serves 4-6

Finely grate rutabaga and carrot. Combine ingredients together in a mixing bowl and toss well. Cover and chill until needed.

Celery & apple salad

A really crunchy salad with an unusual dressing.

Celery, head of 1
Dessert apples 2
Honey & lemon dressing *(see page 89)* 1 recipe
Salt & pepper to taste

Serves 4-6

Slice celery and apples. Combine all ingredients and toss well. Adjust seasoning to taste.

Whole wheat mayonnaise

A substantial and nutritious salad which may be made in advance and kept in the refrigerator for a few days.

Wheat berries 1 cup
Medium-sized carrots 1 to 2
Small onion ½
Mayonnaise *(see page 87)* ½ cup
Salt & pepper to taste

Serves 6

Cook wheat in boiling water until just tender (30-45 minutes, depending on taste). Drain and let cool. Grate carrots and finely chop onion. Mix all ingredients together and toss well. Adjust seasoning to taste. Cover and chill until needed.

Cooking time may be reduced by soaking the wheat, preferably overnight.

Hawaiian rice salad

An exciting combination of flavor and texture.

Long-grain brown rice ½ cup
French dressing *(see page 87)* 4 tbsp
Small pineapple ½
Medium-sized green pepper ½
Salt & pepper to taste

Serves 4

Cook rice in boiling water until tender—about 35 minutes. Drain and let cool, then toss in the French dressing. Cut flesh from pineapple and dice it. Chop green pepper and add to rice with pineapple. Adjust seasoning to taste.

Creamy beet salad

Small raw beets 4
Medium-sized parsnips 2
Chopped parsley 3 tbsp
Sour cream ½ cup
Cider vinegar 2 tbsp
Salt & pepper to taste

Serves 6

Grate beets and parsnips together, and add parsley. Combine remaining ingredients, then mix together with vegetables. Toss well.

Leek salad

Leeks are an unusual vegetable to use in a salad but very quick to prepare and combined with the other ingredients make a very colorful salad.

Large leeks, well trimmed 2
Small red pepper 1
Walnuts, chopped 3 tbsp
Lemon, grated rind & juice of 1
Mayonnaise or French dressing
   (see page 87) 6 tbsp
Salt & pepper to taste

Serves 4-6

Very finely shred leeks, then blanch in boiling water 2 minutes, drain, and cool. Slice red pepper. Put leeks, pepper, and walnuts in a salad bowl. Mix lemon rind and juice with mayonnaise and toss the salad. Adjust seasoning to taste.

Italian pasta salad

Whole wheat pasta rings 2 cups
Medium-sized red pepper 1
Black olives ½ cup
Chopped parsley 3 tbsp
French dressing *(see page 87)*
   4 tbsp
Garlic clove, crushed 1
Salt & pepper to taste

Serves 4-6

Cook pasta rings in boiling water about 15 minutes, or until just tender. Drain and rinse in cold water. Dice red pepper and place in a salad bowl with pasta, olives, and parsley. Mix French dressing with garlic and pour over salad. Toss well. Adjust seasoning to taste.

If pasta rings are not available, use any other small pasta shape, such as broken macaroni.

Bulghur salad

Bulghur makes a light but substantial base for this salad.

Bulghur 1⅓ cups
Small green pepper 1
Scallions, chopped
   2 tbsp
Chopped parsley 3 tbsp
Soy sauce 3 tbsp
French dressing *(see page 87)*
   6 tbsp
Salt & pepper to taste

Serves 6

Place bulghur in a mixing bowl and pour 1½ cups boiling water over it. Fork through from time to time and let cool. Chop green pepper. Fluff up bulghur with a fork, then add remaining ingredients and mix well. Adjust seasoning to taste. Cover and chill until needed.

Celery, cucumber & grape salad

Celery sticks 4
Cucumber ½
Red grapes 1¼ cups

Dressing
Natural yogurt ½ cup
Honey 1 tsp
Dijon mustard 1 tsp
Salt & pepper to taste

Serves 4-6

Chop celery, slice cucumber, halve grapes and remove seeds. Put all the salad ingredients together in a bowl. Mix together ingredients for dressing and season well with salt and pepper. Pour over salad and toss.

Cauliflower, date & banana salad

The crunchy texture of cauliflower combined with the delicate fruit flavors in a tangy dressing produces a delightful salad—good on its own or as part of a salad selection.

Cauliflower 1
Dates, pitted ½ cup
Bananas 2
Mayonnaise *(see page 87)*
   ½ cup
Lemon, grated rind & juice of 1

Serves 4-6

Break cauliflower into florets, then steam 5 minutes. Cool quickly. Chop dates and slice bananas. Mix mayonnaise, lemon rind, and juice together. Combine all the ingredients in a salad bowl and serve.

Green pepper & orange salad

A perfect summer salad, both colorful and refreshing. For a special occasion arrange the tossed salad on a bed of lettuce and garnish with sprigs of fresh mint.

Medium-sized green peppers 2
Large oranges 2
Small onion 1
French dressing *(see page 87)*
   4 tbsp

Serves 4-6

Shred peppers, peel oranges, remove white membrane, and chop flesh. Cut onion into thin rings. Combine all ingredients in a bowl. Toss well, cover, and chill until needed.

Alfalfa salad

Sprouted alfalfa *(see page 27)* 4
   cups
Mung beansprouts 1 cup
Creamy paprika dressing *(see
   page 88)* 6 tbsp

Serves 4

Mix alfalfa and mung beansprouts together. Just before serving toss in dressing.

Taboullah

Originating in the Middle East, this salad is best made with fresh mint to bring out its full flavor.

Cracked wheat 1⅓ cups
Medium-sized onion 1
Fresh mint, chopped (or dried mint) 1 tbsp
Chopped parsley 6 tbsp
Piquant dressing *(see page 88)* ½ cup

Serves 6

Place cracked wheat in bowl and pour over sufficient boiling water to cover. Let soak ½ hour. Drain and rinse well. Finely chop onion. Combine all the ingredients together and toss well into dressing. Cover and chill until needed.

This will keep for several days in a refrigerator.

Endive & oranges with cheese dressing

Medium heads of endive 2
Medium-sized oranges 3
Chopped parsley to garnish

Dressing
French dressing *(see page 87)* 2 tbsp
Skim milk soft cheese 4 tbsp

Serves 4-6

Cut the bottom half of each head of endive into slices and separate the top half into individual leaves. Peel oranges, remove any white membrane and slice thinly. Reserve any juice. Combine all the endive and orange in a bowl. Sprinkle with parsley. Using a fork, mix together French dressing and soft cheese until smooth, then stir in orange juice. Pour over salad and serve at once.

Green bean salad

Green (string) beans 3 cups
Piquant dressing *(see page 88)* ½ cup
Medium-sized tomatoes 1 to 2

Serves 4-6

Top and tail beans. Steam about 20 minutes, or until just tender. While beans are still warm, pour dressing over them. Chop tomato and add to beans. Cover and let cool. Chill until needed.

Green salad

Green salad is served every day in Cranks restaurants. To vary the salad use an equal quantity of spinach, curly endive, or other salad green to replace the lettuce.

Medium lettuce 1
Small onion 1
Alfalfa sprouts 1 cup
French dressing *(see page 87)*

Serves 4-6

Wash, dry, and shred lettuce. Cut onion into fine rings. Place salad ingredients in a large bowl. Toss well with sufficient French dressing to coat.

Flageolet bean salad

Delicate shades of green make this a most attractive salad, best made in advance to allow the flavors to blend.

Flageolet beans (young, green
  kidney beans) soaked
  overnight 1 cup
Lemon, grated rind & juice of 1
Oil 4 tbsp
Garlic clove, crushed 1
Chopped parsley 3 tbsp
Salt & pepper to taste

Serves 4

Cook beans in boiling water about 1 hour, or until just tender, and drain well. Combine remaining ingredients and pour over beans. Cover and marinate several hours. Adjust seasoning to taste.

Tomato salad

For this salad choose firm, good quality tomatoes and cut them with a serrated knife to give even slices. This recipe is ideal as a starter served with chunks of warm whole wheat bread.

Tomatoes 1 lb
Small onion 1
Chopped parsley 2 tbsp
French dressing *(see page 87)*
  4 tbsp

Serves 4

Thinly slice tomatoes. Cut onion into fine rings. Arrange both on a platter. Sprinkle with chopped parsley and dressing. Cover and chill until needed.

Beansprout salad

Beansprouts have become very popular in the last few years. They are available in many supermarkets, but can be easily sprouted at home for very little cost (see page 27).

Whole peanuts ½ cup
Oil 1 tsp
Salt ½ tsp
Carrot 1 small
Bananas 2
Fresh beansprouts 4 cups
Creamy Paprika dressing *(see page 88)*

Serves 4-6

Put peanuts, oil, and salt in a small ovenproof dish. Mix well, then roast in oven at 400°F about 10 minutes, or until golden. Leave until cold. Grate carrots and slice bananas. Combine with peanuts and beansprouts. Toss in sufficient dressing to moisten.

Cabbage & orange salad

Small white cabbage 1
Oranges 3
Sunflower seeds ½ cup
Chopped parsley 4 tbsp
Natural yogurt ½ cup
Salt & pepper to taste

Serves 6

Finely shred cabbage. Peel oranges, remove all white pith, then cut orange segments away from membrane. Combine cabbage, orange segments, and remaining ingredients. Toss well.

Cucumber, tomato & cheese salad

Large tomatoes 3
Large cucumber ½
Feta cheese 1 cup
French dressing *(see page 87)* 4 tbsp

Serves 4

Chop tomatoes and dice cucumber and cheese. Combine all ingredients together in a bowl and toss well.

Watercress & carrot salad

Everyday ingredients that combine well to give a colorful and light-textured salad.

Bunch of watercress 1
Medium-sized carrots 2 to 3
French dressing *(see page 87)* 3 tbsp

Serves 4

Wash watercress and remove any coarse stems. Coarsely grate carrots. Combine all ingredients and toss well. Serve at once.

Avocado salad

This specialty salad should be arranged on individual plates to serve as a starter or side salad.

Ripe avocados 2
Large tomatoes 2
Small onion ½
French dressing *(see page 87)*
    6 tbsp
Chopped parsley 2 tbsp

Serves 4-6

Halve avocados and remove pits. Peel and slice them, then arrange in a shallow dish. Finely chop tomatoes and onion and combine with remaining ingredients and pour over avocados. Serve at once.

Sweet & sour radishes

An unusual method of preparing radishes, which gives them a piquant flavor. Serve them as part of a selection of salads.

Bunch of radishes 1
Salt 1 tsp
Soy sauce 2 tsp
Cider vinegar 2 tbsp
Raw sugar 2 tbsp
Sesame oil 1 tsp

Serves 4

Trim radishes, then "scratch" surface with the prongs of a fork. Place in a single layer on a plate and sprinkle with salt. Leave for 10 minutes. Wash and dry radishes on paper towels. Combine remaining ingredients and pour over radishes. Cover and marinate several hours.

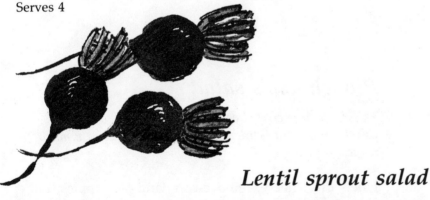

Lentil sprout salad

Lentil sprouts *(see page 27)* 6
    cups
French dressing *(see page 87)*
    4 tbsp
Ground ginger 1 tsp
Large grapefruit 2
Cashew nuts, roasted ½ cup
Salt to taste

Serves 6

Put lentil sprouts in a bowl. Mix French dressing and ground ginger and pour over lentil sprouts. Peel grapefruit, remove all white pith and loosen segments from membrane. Add to salad with their juice. Add cashew nuts and season to taste with salt.

Spiced pepper salad

This can be made in advance and kept for several days in the refrigerator.

Medium-sized red peppers 2
Medium-sized onion 1
Pickling spice 1 tbsp
Mushrooms 1 cup
French dressing *(see page 87)*
    ½ cup

Serves 4-6

Slice peppers and onion. Tie pickling spice in a small piece of cheesecloth. Place vegetables in a bowl with pickling spice and pour boiling water over. Let stand 10 minutes, then drain. Slice and add mushrooms. Bring French dressing to a boil and pour over. Cover and marinate. Remove pickling spice before serving.

Turmeric rice salad

Long-grain brown rice ¾ cup
Golden seedless raisins ½ cup
Turmeric ½ tsp
Garlic clove, crushed 1
French dressing *(see page 87)*
    4 tbsp
Salt & pepper to taste
Chopped parsley to garnish

Serves 4

Cook rice in boiling water 30-35 minutes, or until just tender. Drain. Combine raisins, turmeric, garlic, and French dressing. Pour over rice and stir well. Cover and refrigerate until needed. Fork through, adjust seasoning to taste, and sprinkle with chopped parsley before serving.

Ploughman's salad

This recipe was created as a main meal salad to serve at Cranks in Covent Garden Market and has become a much requested favorite.

Cheddar cheese ½ lb
Green eating apples 3
Onion, finely-chopped 1 tbsp
Parsley, chopped 2 tbsp
Natural yogurt 4 tbsp
French dressing *(see page 87)*
    4 tbsp

Serves 4-6

Finely dice cheese, remove core, and dice apples. Put cheese, apples, onion, and parsley in a mixing bowl. Whisk together natural yogurt and French dressing until evenly mixed, then pour over salad. Mix well.

Tangy zucchini salad

Small zucchini 1 lb
Lemon, grated rind & juice of 1
Garlic clove, crushed 1
Oil 3 tbsp
Salt & pepper to taste

Serves 4

Thinly slice zucchini. Pour boiling water over and leave 5 minutes. Drain. Combine remaining ingredients and pour over zucchini. Adjust seasoning to taste. Cover and let cool.

Tzatziki salad

A salad with a cool refreshing flavor.

Cucumber 1
Garlic cloves 2
Natural yogurt 1 cup
Fresh mint, chopped 1 tbsp
Parsley, chopped 1 tbsp
Salt to taste
Paprika to taste

Serves 4-6

Dice cucumber and crush garlic cloves. Combine garlic, yogurt, mint, and parsley and add cucumber. Season to taste with salt and paprika.

DRESSINGS & SAUCES

A dressing on a salad can give scope for creative artistry, but one shouldn't lose sight of the fact that its prime purpose is to coat the lettuce leaves or pieces of sliced and chopped vegetables with a film of oil to prevent oxidation and the consequent loss of food value, crispness, and flavor.

A badly flavored or a badly seasoned dressing can spoil what would otherwise have been a good salad, so it needs to be prepared with thought and care. It is essential to follow a basic recipe for correct consistency, but of course personal preferences must come into play. Try experimenting with fresh herbs and spices when making both mayonnaise and French dressing. Remember that there are many other dressings as well as these two classics that can be used. Try to match the dressing to the salad—a "heavy" salad is often better with a "light" dressing; in other words, rice with piquant dressing rather than mayonnaise is more appetizing.

The purpose of sauces is to moisten food and to add interest and flavor, and this of course applies equally to vegetarian whole food cooking. Basic white sauce can be made with 100% whole wheat flour, which gives the sauce a slightly off-white color and unusual flavor. When it comes to a savory brown sauce, or the vegetarian alternative to a meat-based gravy, the basic flavor comes from vegetables, yeast extracts, or soy sauce and seaweed. Like salad dressings, sauces are added to a meal to improve the overall quality and appearance, so care in preparation is essential—a poor sauce is almost worse than no sauce!

French dressing

Lemons, juice of 2
Cider or wine vinegar 4 tbsp
Salt 1½ tsp
Pepper ½ tsp
Dijon mustard 1 tbsp
Raw sugar (optional) 2 tsp
Oil 2 cups

Makes about 2¼ cups

Method 1
Put lemon juice, vinegar, salt, pepper, mustard, and sugar in a jar. Whisk with a fork until evenly blended; then slowly work in oil.

Method 2
Put all ingredients together in a blender and blend a few seconds.

Method 3
Shake all ingredients together in a screw-topped jar. Store in the refrigerator.

Mayonnaise

Organic egg 1
Salt ½ tsp
Dijon mustard ½ tsp
Cider or wine vinegar 2 tsp
Oil

Makes about 1 cup

Break egg into a blender. Add salt, mustard, and vinegar. Blend 10 seconds. While blender is switched on, slowly feed in oil through lid. As oil is added, mayonnaise will become thick.

To make mayonnaise by hand, beat egg, salt, mustard, and vinegar together in a bowl using a wooden spoon or whisk, add oil, *drop by drop*, until half the oil has been used. Continue adding in very small quantities until all the oil has been incorporated.

Sour cream dressing

A tangy cream dressing particularly good with raw vegetables.

Sour cream ½ cup
Garlic clove, crushed 1
Cider or wine vinegar 1 tbsp
Dijon mustard 1 tsp
Salt & pepper to taste

Makes about ½ cup

Combine ingredients together. Adjust seasoning to taste with salt and pepper.

Piquant dressing

A welcome change from French dressing.

Oil ¾ cup
Vinegar ¾ cup
Water ½ cup
Scallions or chives, chopped 2
    tbsp
Raw sugar 2 tsp
Paprika 1 tsp
Soy sauce 2 tsp
Salt ½ tsp
Dijon mustard ½ tsp
Pepper to taste

Makes about 2¼ cups

Shake all ingredients together in a screw-topped jar.
Refrigerate and use as needed.

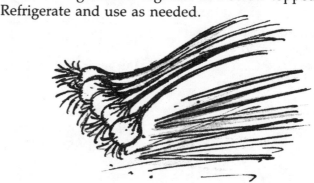

Creamy paprika dressing

Raw sugar 1 tsp
Paprika 2 tsp
Salt 1 tsp
Cider or wine vinegar 4 tbsp
Organic egg 1
Oil ¾ cup

Makes about 1 cup

Combine sugar and seasonings. Add vinegar and egg.
Beat well. Add oil 1 tsp at a time until about
one-quarter has been used. Slowly add remaining oil,
beating well between each addition.

Alternatively, use the blender method as for
MAYONNAISE *(see page 87).*

Yogurt dressing

*A sharp and tangy dressing—not just for the weight
conscious!*

Natural yogurt ½ cup
Raw sugar or honey ½ tsp
Lemon, grated rind & juice of ½
Onion or scallion, finely
    chopped 1 tbsp
Salt & pepper to taste

Makes about ½ cup

Combine all ingredients together in a jar or bowl until
evenly mixed. Season to taste.

Honey & lemon dressing

An ideal dressing for the weight-conscious. It combines well with fruit-based salads.

Lemon, juice of 1
Honey 2 tbsp
Salt & pepper to taste

Makes about 4 tbsp

Whisk ingredients together with a fork.

Nut cream

Use as an alternative to cream on breakfast cereal or stewed or fresh fruit.

Whole blanched almonds or
  cashews ¾ cup
Warm water ½ to 1 cup
Honey to taste
Lemon rind (optional)

Makes about 1 cup

Grind nuts in a coffee mill, then transfer to a bowl. Gradually beat in water to give a smooth, creamy paste. (Add sufficient water to give required consistency.) Sweeten with honey to taste. Add a little grated lemon rind if wished.

Basic "white" sauce

Whole wheat flour produces an oatmeal-colored sauce, rich in flavor and far removed from the bleached look of refined flour sauces. Variations in color and texture can be produced by using alternatives, such as barley or cornmeal.

Butter or margarine 4 tbsp
100% whole wheat flour ½ cup
Milk 2 cups
Salt & pepper to taste

Makes about 2 cups

Melt butter in a saucepan. Off the heat, stir in flour, then cook 1-2 minutes, stirring continuously. Slowly stir in milk until it is evenly blended. Bring to a boil, reduce heat, and simmer 2-3 minutes. Adjust seasoning to taste.

VARIATIONS
Cheese Add ½ tsp mustard powder with flour. Stir in 1 cup grated Cheddar cheese at the end of cooking. Do not boil after adding cheese.

Parsley Add 6 tbsp chopped parsley after milk.

Tomato sauce

An essential sauce in vegetarian cooking. Make this regularly and store in the refrigerator until ready to use it.

Medium-sized onion 1
Medium-sized tomatoes 2 to 3
Butter or margarine 2 tbsp
Vegetable stock or water 1 cup
Garlic clove, crushed 1
Tomato paste 1 tbsp
Basil ½ tsp
Salt & pepper to taste

Makes about 2 cups

Chop onion and tomatoes. Melt butter in a large saucepan and sauté onion gently until transparent. Add remaining ingredients, bring to a boil, then reduce heat and simmer uncovered 20 minutes. Serve with pasta, rice dishes, and savoury pies.

Curry sauce

Medium-sized onion 1
Medium-sized carrots 2
Medium-sized cooking apples 2
Butter or margarine 4 tbsp
Curry powder 1 tbsp
100% whole wheat flour 3 tbsp
Golden seedless raisins, soaked
   for 1 hour ⅓ cup
Milk 1 cup
Vegetable stock 1 cup

Makes about 3 cups

Finely chop onion, carrot, and apple. Melt butter and sauté prepared vegetables and apple until onion is transparent. Stir in curry powder and flour and cook 2 minutes, stirring. Add remaining ingredients, bring to a boil, reduce heat, cover, and simmer ½ hour.

Serve with hard-boiled eggs or diced cooked vegetables on a bed of boiled rice.

Savoury brown sauce

Butter or margarine 4 tbsp
Large onion 1
100% whole wheat flour ½ cup
Vegetable stock 2 cups
Vegex 1 tbsp
Pepper to taste

Makes 2 cups

Melt butter. Skin and finely chop onion and sauté until golden brown. Stir in flour and cook 2 minutes, stirring occasionally. Pour in stock and Vegex, stirring. Bring to a boil, reduce heat, cover, and simmer 10 minutes. Adjust seasoning to taste. Serve with baked savoury dishes and nut rissoles.

If wished, strain sauce or blend in a blender before serving.

SAVOURIES

According to the dictionary, the word "savoury" means "appetizing, salty or spiced, having relish." In a meat meal when there is a savoury it is a small dish, meeting this definition, served at the beginning or end of the meal. What a vegetarian does is to elevate the importance of the savoury to the central position of the meal to replace the meat or fish.

Most hotels or restaurants faced with a vegetarian will be hard put to offer them anything more for a main dish than an omelette, and how boring this can become! Finding an alternative to meat, poultry, or fish, which are so simple to provide, certainly does call for more imagination and more work, but the results can be creatively very rewarding, and the flavorful dishes come as a great surprise when first experienced by meat eaters.

Cranks must have opened quite a few eyes to the extraordinary wealth of possible flavors and dishes that can be produced by using only nuts and legumes, eggs and cheeses, rice, vegetables and cereals.

In recent years textured soy protein (TSP) has come on the market with a meat-like texture and in a variety of meat-like forms. These are often sold with chemical coloring and flavoring aimed at getting as close as possible to the different meats and are therefore, with good reason, shunned by vegetarians or those concerned about the dangers of food additives. But the plain variety, carefully flavored, can be very pleasant to eat and has its place as an alternative food, and it certainly helps those starting on a vegetarian diet to make the transition more easily. For this reason we have included some recipes using it.

We believe that vegetarian savoury dishes should be thought of as meals in their own right, containing the important food values. There is endless scope for experimenting with the making of savouries from a whole food vegetarian larder, and we hope that our recipes will form just a starting point for your voyage of discovery!

Brown rice risotto

Medium-sized onion 1
Medium-sized green pepper 1
Butter or margarine 2 tbsp
Oil 3 tbsp
Broken cashew nuts ½ cup
Medium-sized tomatoes 4
Long-grain brown rice, cooked
   1⅓ cups
Garlic clove, crushed 1
Salt & pepper to taste

Serves 4

Chop onion and slice pepper. Heat butter and oil in a large saucepan. Add green pepper, onion, and cashews and sauté until vegetables are just tender, stirring occasionally. Chop tomatoes and add to pan with rice and garlic. Continue stirring over a gentle heat until rice is heated through. Adjust seasoning to taste.

Mushroom & potato pie

A delicious mixture of mushrooms in sauce topped with creamed potatoes—a Cranks favorite.

Potatoes 2 lb
Celery sticks 4
Medium-sized onion 1
Mushrooms 1 lb
Butter or margarine 6 tbsp
Milk 4 tbsp
Garlic cloves, crushed 2
Cornstarch 1½ tbsp
Milk ¾ cup
Chopped parsley 2 tbsp
Dried thyme 1 tsp
Lemon juice 2 tsp
Salt & pepper to taste

Serves 4-6

Cook potatoes in boiling water until tender. Grate celery and chop onion and mushrooms. Drain potatoes, add 2 tbsp butter and 4 tbsp milk, then mash until creamy. Season well. Melt remaining butter in a large saucepan. Add celery and onion and cook gently until onion is transparent. Add mushrooms and garlic, and cook, stirring occasionally, 5 minutes. Blend cornstarch with a little milk, stir in remaining milk and stir into mushrooms. Add parsley, thyme, and lemon juice, and season to taste. Simmer gently 5 minutes. Turn mixture into an ovenproof serving dish. Top with mashed potato and place under a broiler until heated through and golden, or place in the oven at 375°F about 20 minutes.

Vegetable fricassée

This versatile recipe can be served on a bed of freshly boiled rice or in individual ovenproof dishes topped with grated cheese and breadcrumbs and bubbled under broiler. Alternatively, use as a pie filling.

Rutabaga 2 cups
Medium-sized potatoes 2

Cut vegetables into ¾" chunks. Break cauliflower into large florets. Bring stock to a boil in a large saucepan,

Medium-sized carrots 2 to 3
Large leek 1
Small cauliflower ½
Vegetable stock or water 2 cups
Butter or margarine 4 tbsp
100% whole wheat flour ½ cup
Milk
Chopped parsley 6 tbsp
Lemon juice 1 tsp
Salt & pepper to taste

Serves 4-6

add rutabaga and carrots, return to a boil, then add potatoes and simmer 5 minutes. Add leeks and cauliflower and cook a further 3-5 minutes, until just tender but still crisp. Drain, reserving stock. Keep vegetables warm. Melt butter in the saucepan, stir in flour, and cook 1 minute. Mix stock with milk. Add stock and milk mixture, stirring, and bring to a boil. Reduce heat, add remaining ingredients, and simmer 2-3 minutes. Pour sauce over vegetables and serve at once.

Macaroni in tomato sauce

This recipe also works with any other small pasta shapes.

Whole wheat macaroni 1½ cups
Medium-sized red or green
    pepper 1
Small zucchini 2
Butter or margarine 2 tbsp
Tomato sauce (*see page 90*)
    1 recipe

Serves 4

Cook macaroni in boiling salted water about 15 minutes, or until just tender. Drain. Chop pepper and slice zucchini. Melt butter in a saucepan, add peppers and zucchini, and sauté about 3 minutes, or until tender but still crisp. Bring tomato sauce to a boil, add macaroni and vegetables, and heat to serving temperature.

Cranks nut roast

For a main course this is the ideal dish to present to anyone who is doubtful about the question of whether vegetarian food is satisfying, or exciting, or nutritious enough!

The actual preparation is easy, and the time taken not excessive, and there are, of course, many variations that can be attempted at a later date, once the basic dish has been mastered.

Basic recipe
Medium-sized onion 1
Butter or margarine 2 tbsp
Mixed nuts, i.e. peanuts,
    walnuts, cashews, etc. 1½
    cups
Whole wheat bread 4 slices
Vegetable stock or water
    1 cup
Vegex 2 tsp
Mixed herbs 1 tsp
Salt & pepper to taste

Serves 4-6

Chop onions and sauté in butter until transparent. Grind nuts and bread together in a blender or coffee grinder until quite fine. Heat stock and Vegex to boiling point, then combine all the ingredients together and mix well. Turn into a greased shallow baking dish, level the surface, sprinkle with a few breadcrumbs, and bake at 350°F 30 minutes, or until golden brown.

VARIATIONS
Nut loaf with cheese and tomato layer Follow the basic recipe for NUT ROAST, but add only 3-4 tbsp of stock to give a firm mixture. Press half the mixture into a greased 1 lb loaf pan. Cover with 2 sliced tomatoes and 2 oz grated cheese and top with remaining mixture. Bake as for NUT ROAST. Allow to cool in the pan, then remove carefully. Wrap in plastic wrap or waxed paper and put in the refrigerator. Cut into slices.

Rissoles Make up as for NUT LOAF but shape mixture into 6 round cakes, coat with whole wheat breadcrumbs and sauté in shallow oil 3-5 minutes each side until golden brown. Serve hot or cold.

Cottage pie This is the Cranks vegetarian variation of Shepherd's Pie. Make up as for NUT ROAST, but add sufficient stock to give a loose texture, spoon into an ovenproof dish, and top with 1½ lb potatoes that have been boiled and mashed with a little milk and butter, pepper, and salt. Bake at 400°F 20-30 minutes, or until potato is crisp and golden.

continued

Jacket eggs Follow the recipe for NUT LOAF. Shell 4 hard-boiled organic eggs and let sit until cold. Encase the eggs in NUT LOAF mixture. Roll in fresh whole wheat breadcrumbs and deep fry until golden. Drain and serve hot or cold.

Savoury carrot layer

A savoury custard with two contrasting layers–a base of flavorful carrot purée topped with a cheese custard.

For the base
Carrots 1 lb
Vegetable stock or water
    ½ to 1 cup
Butter or margarine 2 tbsp
Chopped parsley 2 tbsp
Soy sauce 1 tsp
Salt & pepper to taste

For the topping
Butter or margarine 2 tbsp
100% whole wheat flour ¼ cup
Milk ½ cup
Organic eggs, beaten 3
Cheddar cheese, grated ¾ cup

Serves 4

Grate carrots and put in a saucepan with ½ cup vegetable stock and the butter. Cover and simmer about 15 minutes until carrots are really tender. Add parsley and soy sauce and blend mixture in a blender until fairly smooth, adding a little more stock if necessary. Season to taste. Spread mixture in the base of a greased ovenproof dish.

Melt butter in a saucepan, stir in flour, and cook 1 minute. Stir in milk and continue simmering a further 2 minutes. Off the heat, beat in eggs and then cheese. Adjust seasoning to taste. Pour over carrot mixture, then bake at 350°F about 45 minutes, or until just set. Serve at once.

Tomato & cheese pizza

Bread dough (*see page 169*) ⅓
    recipe
Large onion 1
Oil 2 tbsp
Tomatoes 1 lb
Garlic clove, crushed 1
Tomato paste 2 tbsp
Basil ½ tsp
Oregano ½ tsp
Salt & pepper to taste
Button mushrooms 4
Green pepper ½
Black olives 12
Cheddar cheese, grated ½ cup

Serves 4

Knead dough lightly, then roll out to a 12″ round or four 6″ rounds on a lightly floured surface. Place dough on a greased baking sheet, cover with pieces of greased plastic wrap and leave in a warm place ½ hour to rise. Chop onion, heat oil in a saucepan, and sauté onion until transparent. Reserve 2 tomatoes, chop the rest and add to the pan with the garlic, tomato paste, herbs, and seasoning. Simmer gently, stirring occasionally, until mixture is pulpy. Wash mushrooms and cut each into 4 slices. Wash and trim pepper and cut into 12 chunks. Spread tomato mixture over dough base. Decorate with olives, mushroom slices, pepper, and remaining tomatoes, cut into wedges, and sprinkle with cheese. Bake at 425°F about 25 minutes. Small pizzas will take about 15 minutes.

Macaroni cheese with vegetables

A variation on the classic recipe—other vegetables may be substitutes as wished.

Medium-sized carrots 1 to 2
Small zucchini 2
Celery sticks 4
Whole wheat macaroni 1½ cups
Vegetable stock or water 1 cup
Butter or margarine 4 tbsp
100% whole wheat flour ½ cup
Milk
Cheddar cheese 1 cup
Salt & pepper to taste

Serves 4

Finely slice vegetables. Cook macaroni in boiling salted water about 15 minutes, or until just tender. Drain in a colander or strainer. Put prepared vegetables and stock in a saucepan. Bring to a boil, then simmer 5 minutes and drain, reserving stock. Mix up to 2 cups stock with milk. Melt butter in a saucepan, stir in flour, and cook 1 minute. Stir in stock and cook a further few minutes. Off the heat, stir in ¾ cup cheese and season to taste. Add macaroni and vegetables to sauce. Spoon into a flame-proof serving dish, sprinkle with remaining cheese, and place under the broiler until golden.

Mushroom "burgers"

Medium-sized onion 1
Mushrooms 2 to 3 cups
Oil 2 tbsp
100% whole wheat flour ½ cup
Water ½ cup
Vegex 1 tsp
Lemon juice 1 tsp
Ground nutmeg to taste
Fresh whole wheat breadcrumbs
    1½ cups
Organic egg, hardboiled, shelled
    & finely chopped 1
Salt & pepper to taste

To coat
Organic eggs, beaten 2
100% dried whole wheat
    breadcrumbs 1 cup
Oil for frying

Makes 8 "burgers"

Chop onion and mushrooms. Heat oil in a saucepan and sauté onion until transparent. Add mushrooms and cook 1-2 minutes, stirring. Stir in flour, then the water, Vegex, lemon juice, and nutmeg. Simmer gently 5 minutes, stirring frequently. Off the heat, stir in breadcrumbs and chopped egg, then adjust seasoning to taste. Let sit until cold. With floured hands shape mixture into 8 patties, dip in beaten egg and then in breadcrumbs. Sauté in shallow oil over medium heat about 5 minutes, or until each side is golden brown. Drain on paper towels. Serve hot or cold.

Moussaka

This a vegetarian version of the traditional Greek moussaka using TSP (Textured Soy Protein) instead of minced meat.

Medium-sized onion 1
Oil 6 tbsp
Garlic clove 1
Mushrooms ½ cup
Tomatoes 2
Tomato paste 1 tbsp
Water ½ cup
Vegex 1 tsp
TSP minced style ⅔ cup
Vegetable stock cube 1
Parsley, chopped 1 tbsp
Large eggplant 1
100% whole wheat flour 2 tbsp
Cheddar cheese, grated ½ cup
Organic eggs 3
Natural yogurt ½ cup

Serves 4

Chop onion, mushrooms, tomatoes and thinly slice eggplant. Heat 2 tbsp oil in a saucepan and sauté onion until transparent. Add crushed garlic, mushrooms, tomatoes, tomato paste, water, Vegex, TSP, stock cube, and parsley. Stir well, bring to a boil, reduce heat, and simmer, covered, 10 minutes. Dust eggplant slices in flour, then sauté in remaining oil until soft. In an ovenproof dish layer eggplant and TSP mixture finishing with a layer of eggplant. Sprinkle with cheese. Whisk together eggs and yogurt and pour over pie. Bake at 350°F 35-40 minutes, or until golden brown.

Spicy chickpeas

Chickpeas are very much underrated, although they can give a good protein base as well as an unusual flavor and texture to savoury dishes.

Chickpeas, soaked overnight 1 cup
Butter or margarine 2 tbsp
Medium-sized onion 1
Tomatoes 1 lb
Spinach 2 cups
Ground cumin 1 tsp
Oregano 1 tsp
Paprika 1 tsp
Cheddar cheese, grated 1 cup
Salt to taste
Natural yogurt to garnish
Paprika to garnish

Serves 4-6

Place pre-soaked chickpeas in a saucepan, just cover with water, and simmer about 45 minutes, or until tender. Drain, reserving ⅔ cups cooking liquor. Measure out ½ cup chickpeas and blend in a blender with cooking liquid until smooth. Chop onion and tomatoes, and shred spinach. Melt butter in a saucepan and sauté onion until transparent. Add cumin and whole chickpeas, and cook, stirring, 2 minutes. Stir in spinach, tomatoes, and blended chickpeas, herbs, and seasonings. Bring to a boil, reduce heat, and simmer 5 minutes. Off the heat, stir in cheese until melted. Adjust seasoning to taste.

Serve at once topped with yogurt and sprinkled with a little paprika.

Eggs Florentine

Spinach 1 lb
Butter or margarine 4 tbsp
Salt & pepper to taste
Ground nutmeg to taste
Small onion 1
100% whole wheat flour ¼ cup
Mustard powder 1 tsp
Milk 1 cup
Cheddar cheese, grated 1 cup
Organic eggs, hardboiled & shelled 4
Brown rice, freshly cooked ⅔ cup
Toasted breadcrumbs 1 tbsp

Serves 4

Shred spinach. Melt half the butter in a saucepan, add spinach, and cook over medium heat a few minutes, stirring frequently, until just tender. Season with salt, pepper, and nutmeg. Keep warm. Chop onion. Melt remaining butter in a saucepan and sauté onion until transparent. Stir in flour and mustard and cook 1 minute. Add milk, stirring, bring to boil and simmer a few minutes. Off the heat, stir in cheese. Arrange rice in a warmed serving dish and spoon spinach in the center. Arrange halved eggs on top and pour sauce over eggs. Sprinkle breadcrumbs over and serve at once.

Eggplant Parmesan

A hearty and warming savoury with an Italian flavor.

Potatoes 1 lb
Eggplant 1 lb
Oil ½ cup
Butter or margarine 4 tbsp
Medium-sized onion 1
Tomatoes 4
100% whole wheat flour 2 tbsp
Milk ½ cup
Garlic clove, crushed 1
Basil ½ tsp
Oregano ½ tsp
Salt & pepper to taste
Parmesan cheese 3 tbsp
Whole wheat breadcrumbs
   3 tbsp
Chopped parsley to garnish

Serves 4-6

Cut potatoes into large pieces and cook in boiling water about 10 minutes, or until just tender. Drain, reserving 1 cup cooking liquid. Dice eggplant and chop onion and tomatoes. Heat oil and sauté eggplant until golden and tender. Melt half the butter and sauté onion until transparent. Add tomatoes, stir in flour, and cook 1 minute. Add potato liquid, milk, garlic, herbs, and seasoning. Bring to a boil, reduce heat, and simmer 15-20 minutes. Spoon potatoes and eggplant into a warmed serving dish. Spoon over tomato sauce. Mix together breadcrumbs and Parmesan cheese and sprinkle over the sauce. Dot with remaining butter. Place in the oven at 400°F about 20 minutes, or until heated through. Sprinkle with chopped parsley.

Millet & vegetable gratinée

The contrasting flavors and textures of millet and vegetables provide a satisfying savoury dish.

Millet ½ cup
Water 2¼ cups
Butter or margarine 6 tbsp
Medium-sized leeks 2
Large carrot 1
Celery sticks 4
100% whole wheat flour ¼ cup
Milk 2¼ cups
Chopped parsley 3 tbsp
Sage 1 tsp
Lemon, grated rind & juice of ½
Salt & pepper to taste
Cheddar cheese, grated 1 cup

Serves 4-6

Cook millet in measured boiling water until just tender and all the water has been absorbed. Slice leeks, grate the carrot, and finely slice the celery. Melt 4 tbsp butter in a saucepan, add vegetables, and sauté 10-15 minutes, stirring frequently. Add millet and stir over very gentle heat to keep warm. Meanwhile, melt remaining butter in a saucepan. Stir in flour and cook 1 minute. Stir in milk, herbs, lemon rind and juice, and bring to a boil. Reduce heat and simmer 2 minutes. Pour it over vegetables and stir well. Add salt and pepper if needed. Transfer to a warmed serving dish, sprinkle with cheese, and broil until golden brown.

Lentil & buckwheat slice

Delicious served hot with green vegetables or cold as part of a packed lunch.

Buckwheat ⅔ cup
Medium-sized onion 1
Medium-sized carrot 1
Oil 2 tbsp
Red lentils 1 cup
Vegetable stock or water 3¾ cups
Chopped parsley 2 tbsp
Rosemary, powdered ½ tsp
Vegex 1 tsp
Salt & pepper to taste
Nutmeg to taste

Serves 6

Toast buckwheat until golden brown. Chop onion and carrot. Heat oil in a saucepan and sauté onion and carrot until onion is transparent. Add buckwheat and lentils, and then remaining ingredients. Bring to a boil, reduce heat, and simmer about ½ hour, or until all liquid is absorbed. Press mixture into a greased 10″ pie pan, and bake at 400°F ½ hour. Serve hot or cold in wedges with chutney.

Golden vegetable layer

Rutabaga 1 lb
Large potato 1
Large carrot 1
Butter or margarine 4 tbsp
Salt & pepper to taste
Tomato sauce *(see page 90)* 1 recipe
Chopped parsley to garnish

Serves 4

Chop rutabaga, potato, and carrot and steam 20-25 minutes, or until just tender. Boil tomato sauce until it becomes a thick purée. Keep warm. Roughly mash vegetables (do not let them become smooth) with butter and season generously with salt and pepper. Spoon mixture into a warmed serving dish, top with tomato sauce, and sprinkle with chopped parsley. Serve at once.

This dish could be prepared in advanced and heated through in a medium oven for about ½ hour.

Oriental beansprouts

An exotic blend of ingredients gives the beansprouts an exciting sweet-and-sour flavor.

Medium-sized onion 1
Medium-sized carrot 1
Large green pepper ½
Celery sticks 2
Butter or margarine 2 tbsp
Cucumber ¼
Medium-sized tomatoes 1 to 2
Garlic clove, crushed 1

Chop onion, finely chop carrot and green pepper, thinly slice celery. Melt butter in a large saucepan and add onion, carrot, pepper, and celery, and sauté until onion is transparent. Chop cucumber and tomatoes and add all the remaining ingredients except beansprouts. Bring to a boil, reduce heat, cover, and simmer until vegetables are just tender. Stir in

continued

Pineapple juice
1 cup } blended
together
Cornstarch 1 tbsp
Cider vinegar 3 tbsp
Raw sugar 2 tbsp
Vegetable stock cube 1
Soy sauce 2 tsp
Ground ginger ½ tsp
Ground bay leaf, pinch
Salt & pepper to taste
Beansprouts 6 cups

Serves 4

beansprouts and cook a further 2 minutes. Serve at once.

Mushroom Stroganoff

Large onion 1
Celery sticks 4
Mushrooms 3 cups
Butter or margarine 4 tbsp
100% whole wheat flour 1 tbsp
Water ½ cup
Vegex 1 tsp
Thyme ½ tsp
Ground bay leaf, pinch
Sour cream ½ cup
Salt & pepper to taste
Chopped parsley to garnish

Serves 4

Slice onion, celery, and mushrooms. Melt half the butter in a saucepan, and sauté onion and celery until onion is transparent. Add remaining butter and allow to melt, add mushrooms, and stir occasionally over medium heat 2-3 minutes. Stir in flour, then add water, Vegex, and herbs. Bring to a boil, reduce heat, and simmer, uncovered, 2-3 minutes. Off the heat, stir in sour cream and adjust seasoning to taste. Heat very gently to serving temperature. Serve at once on a bed of freshly cooked rice. Sprinkle with parsley.

Vegetarian goulash

Medium-sized onion 1
Medium-sized zucchini 2
Medium-sized carrots 2
Small white cabbage ½
Oil 3 tbsp
Paprika 1 tbsp
Caraway seeds ½ tsp
Mixed herbs ½ tsp
Nutmeg, pinch
Tomato juice 2 cups
Water 1 cup
Vegetable stock cube 1
Salt to taste
Sour cream or natural yogurt
½ cup

Serves 4-6

Slice onion and zucchini, dice carrots, and finely shred cabbage. Heat oil in a large saucepan and sauté onion and carrot until onion is transparent. Add zucchini and cabbage and cook over medium heat 10 minutes, stirring frequently. Stir in paprika, caraway seeds, herbs, and nutmeg, then add tomato juice, water, and stock cube. Cover and simmer about 20 minutes, or until vegetables are just tender. Add salt if needed. Spoon goulash into a warmed serving dish and drizzle with sour cream or yogurt. Serve at once.

Express cheese custard

Takes only minutes to prepare!

Small onion 1
Whole wheat breadcrumbs 1 cup
Cheddar cheese, grated 1 cup
Organic eggs 2
Dijon mustard 1 tsp
Milk 2 cups
Salt & pepper ¼ tsp of each
Chopped parsley to garnish

Serves 4

Peel and roughly chop onion. Put all the ingredients together in a blender and blend until smooth. Pour mixture into a greased shallow baking dish and bake at 400°F about 45 minutes, until set and golden brown. Sprinkle with chopped parsley.

Curried split peas

Green split peas, soaked
  overnight 1 cup
Medium-sized onion 1
Medium-sized carrots 2
Butter or margarine 4 tbsp
Medium-sized cooking apples 2
Curry powder 1 tbsp
100% whole wheat flour 3 tbsp
Golden seedless raisins, soaked
  for 1 hour ⅓ cup
Milk 1 cup
Salt & pepper to taste
Toasted coconut to garnish

Serves 6

Cover peas with water and bring to a boil. Simmer, covered, about ½ hour. Take off the heat and keep to one side. Finely chop onion and dice carrots. Melt butter in a saucepan and sauté prepared vegetables until onion is transparent. Chop apples. Stir curry powder and flour into sautéed vegetables. Drain peas, reserving 1 cup of cooking liquid and add split peas and liquid to pan with remaining ingredients, except toasted coconut. Bring to a boil, reduce heat, and simmer about ½ hour. Adjust seasoning to taste. Serve on a bed of freshly cooked rice and garnish with toasted coconut.

Navy beans in tomato sauce

A bean stew with a difference.

Navy beans ⅔ cup
Large zucchini 1
Large green pepper 1
Medium-sized onion 1
Medium-sized tomatoes 1 to 2
Butter or margarine 4 tbsp
100% whole wheat flour ¼ cup
Milk 2 cups
Bay leaf 1
Garlic clove, crushed 1
Basil ½ tsp
Salt & pepper to taste

Serves 4-6

Soak beans overnight. Strain, cover with fresh water, bring to a boil, reduce heat, and simmer 2 hours, checking water from time to time. Slice zucchini, cut green pepper into strips, and chop onion and tomatoes. Melt half the butter in a saucepan and sauté zucchini and pepper until just tender. Remove from pan. Add remaining butter to pan and sauté onion until transparent. Stir in flour, and then milk. Bring to a boil, and then reduce heat. Add tomatoes, bay leaf, garlic, and basil, and simmer 10 minutes. Stir in drained beans, zucchini, and pepper. Adjust seasoning to taste. If wished, sprinkle with grated cheese before serving.

Winter hot pot

Medium-sized onion 1
Medium-sized carrots 2 to 3
Medium-sized potato 1
Large parsnip 1
Medium-sized turnip 1
Medium-sized rutabaga 2 to 3
Butter or margarine 4 tbsp
Barley, soaked ¼ cup
Water 3¾ cups
Vegex 1 tbsp
Garlic cloves, chopped 2
Bay leaf 1
Thyme ½ tsp
100% whole wheat flour ¼ cup
Water 2 tbsp
Salt & pepper to taste

Serves 4-6

Chop all the vegetables. Melt butter in a large saucepan and sauté onions and carrots until onions are transparent. Add remaining vegetables, barley, water, Vegex, garlic, bay leaf, and thyme. Bring to a boil, reduce heat, cover, and simmer 15-20 minutes, or until vegetables are just tender. Blend flour and water and stir into hot pot–simmer 2-3 minutes to thicken. Adjust seasoning to taste with salt and pepper.

"Macro" rice

Originally Cranks introduced this recipe to cater to the needs of those on a macrobiotic diet. Since then it has become one of the most popular daily dishes in the restaurants.

Long-grain brown rice 1 cup
Medium-sized onions 2
Oil 4 tbsp
Parsley, chopped 4 tbsp
Soy sauce 2 tbsp
Salt & pepper to taste

Serves 4

Cook rice in boiling water 30-40 minutes, or until just tender. (Halfway through the cooking time, start cooking onions). Slice onions. Heat oil in a frying pan and sauté onions until transparent, without browning them. Add parsley and stir through 1 minute. Drain rice and add to onions in frying pan. Add soy sauce and stir through. Adjust seasoning to taste. Serve at once–or if wished, allow to cool and serve as a salad course.

Savoury Mix

There has always been a need within the vegetarian diet for a protein-based mixture to replace sausage meat and ground beef. Here is Cranks' solution to that need! Use it to fill pies, turnovers, and rolls.

Yellow split peas ½ cup
Medium-sized carrot 1
Medium-sized onion 1
Water 2 cups
Oatmeal 1½ cups
Oil 1 tbsp
Garlic cloves, crushed 2
Vegex 2 tsp
Tomato paste 1 tbsp
Thyme 1 tsp
Sage 1 tsp
Parsley, chopped 2 tbsp
Fresh breadcrumbs 2 cups
Salt & pepper to taste

Makes about 2 lb

Soak peas in water overnight. Grate carrot and onion. Put peas and water in a saucepan with carrot and onion. Bring to a boil, reduce heat, and simmer covered 20 minutes. Add oatmeal and cook a further 10 minutes. Off the heat, stir in remaining ingredients and let cool. Adjust seasoning to taste.

Lentil & cheese wedges

Red lentils 1 cup
Water 2 cups
Large onion 1
Butter or margarine 2 tbsp
Cheddar cheese, grated 1 cup
Mixed herbs 1 tsp
Organic egg 1
Whole wheat breadcrumbs ½
    cup
Salt & pepper to taste

Serves 6

Cook lentils in water until soft and all the liquid has
been absorbed. Chop onion, then melt butter in a
saucepan and sauté onion until transparent. Combine
all the ingredients together and press into an oiled 9″
pie pan. Bake at 375°F 30 minutes. Serve hot or cold,
in wedges.

Surrey raised pie

Makes an impressive centerpiece on a buffet table.

Hot water crust pastry *(see page 181)*
    1 recipe
Savoury mix *(see page 105)*
    ¾ recipe
Tomatoes, sliced 4
Salad ingredients to garnish

Use three-quarters of the pastry to line a 6″ round
cake pan. Place half the savoury mix in base of pan.
Top with sliced tomatoes and finish with a layer of
savoury mix. Roll out remaining pastry and use as top
crust. Seal edges well and make a decorative edge.
Make a hole in the center of the pie. Use trimmings to
make leaves and arrange on top of pie. Bake at 400°F
about 45 minutes. If over-browning, cover pastry with
foil. Allow to cool in the pan, remove carefully, and
serve on a large plate garnished with salad
ingredients.

Soy Mix—using Textured Soy Protein

Using TSP makes this a quickly prepared and easy alternative savoury filling.

Medium-sized onion 1
Butter or margarine 2 tbsp
Medium-sized tomatoes 1 to 2
TSP minced style 1¼ cups
Rice flour ¼ cup
Basil 1 tsp
Vegex 1 tsp
Water ½ cup
Organic egg, beaten 1
Salt & pepper to taste
Fresh whole wheat breadcrumbs
    1 cup

Chop onion and tomatoes, then melt butter in a saucepan and sauté onion until transparent. Add tomatoes and cook a further few minutes until pulpy. Stir in TSP, rice flour, basil, Vegex, and water and simmer gently 5 minutes. Off the heat, stir in beaten egg, season generously with salt and pepper, and stir in breadcrumbs. Use as a pie filling. If wished, add extra stock to give a more moist consistency.

Soy, egg & vegetable pie

Medium-sized carrot 1
Shelled fresh peas, or green
    beans ⅔ cup
Unflavored gelatin 1 tbsp
Vegetable stock 2 cups
Whole wheat shortcrust pastry,
    made with 3½ cups flour (*see
    page 181*)
Soy mix (*see page 107*)
    ½ recipe
Organic eggs, hard boiled &
    shelled 3

Serves 6-8

Dice carrots and steam with peas or beans 5 minutes. Cool. Mix gelatin with a little stock to give a smooth paste; add remaining stock, then simmer 2 minutes. Let cool. Meanwhile, roll out two-thirds of the pastry and use to line 2 lb loaf pan. Layer soy mix and vegetables, arranging whole eggs along length of the pie, in the center. Pour in cooked gelatin until it reaches the top of the pie. Roll out remaining pastry and use as top crust. Seal edges well. Make a large hole in the center. Use pastry trimmings to make leaves and arrange these around the steam hole on top of pie. Bake at 400°F about 40 minutes. Leave in pan until completely cold. Remove carefully and slice.

Soyburgers in salad buns

The whole food answer to the fast food craze!

Soy mix (*see page 107*) ½ recipe
Oil 2 tbsp
Whole wheat buns 4 (*see page 169*)
Butter or margarine 8 tbsp

continued

Shape soy mix into 4 burgers. Sauté gently in a minimum of oil until golden on both sides. Split and butter buns, shred lettuce, and slice tomatoes. Arrange a little shredded lettuce on each bun.

Small lettuce 1
Large tomatoes 2
Mayonnaise *(see page 87)* 4 tbsp

Makes 4

Fill with a soy burger, sliced tomatoes, and mayonnaise.

Buckwheat pancakes

Buckwheat flour is becoming increasingly popular as an alternative to whole wheat flour in pancake batters. The resulting pancakes are dark in color and have the distinctive buckwheat flavor.

Buckwheat flour ½ cup
100% whole wheat flour ½ cup
Salt, pinch
Organic egg 1
Milk 1 cup
Oil or margarine for sautéing

Makes 8-10 pancakes

Put flours and salt into a bowl. Make a well in the center, break egg into the well, then whisk in milk a little at a time, until batter is the consistency of cream. Thin with a little extra milk if necessary. Lightly oil a small frying pan, heat gently, then, holding the pan at an angle, pour in a little of the batter, swirling it round the pan to give a thin layer. Cook over medium heat until batter is set. Turn with a spatula and brown on the second side.

SERVING SUGGESTIONS
Sprinkle with cheese and roll up.
Spoon a little ratatouille in the center and fold up.
Serve with sour cream and honey.

Stir-fried leeks with mushrooms

Small leeks 8
Button mushrooms 1½ lb
Butter or margarine 4 tbsp
Raw sugar ½ tsp
Turmeric ½ tsp
Ground ginger 1 tsp
100% whole wheat flour 4 tbsp
Vegetable stock ¾ cup

Serves 6

Slice leeks and quarter mushrooms. Melt butter in a large frying pan. Add leeks and mushrooms and stir constantly over high heat until vegetables are just tender. Combine remaining ingredients, except flour and stock. Sprinkle flour over vegetables, stir through, then add flavored stock. Bring to a boil, reduce heat, and simmer 5 minutes.

Cauliflower cheese

Medium-sized cauliflower 1
Cheese sauce *(see page 89)*
  1 recipe
Fresh whole wheat breadcrumbs
  4 tbsp
Grated cheese 1 cup

Serves 4

Break cauliflower into large florets. Steam 10-12 minutes, depending on size, or until just tender. Turn into an ovenproof serving dish, spoon over the sauce. Sprinkle with breadcrumbs and cheese and broil until golden.

Buckwheat bake

Truly original in flavor, this really should be tasted—season generously for best results.

Medium-sized onion 1
Tomatoes 4
Oil 2 tbsp
Buckwheat ½ cup
Long-grain rice 2½ tbsp
Water 1 cup
Basil 1 tsp
Salt & pepper to taste

Serves 4-6

Chop onion and tomatoes. Heat oil in a saucepan and sauté onions until transparent. Add tomatoes and stir until softened. Stir in buckwheat and rice and cook 1 minute. Add remaining ingredients. Bring to a boil, reduce heat, cover, and simmer until liquid has been absorbed (about 20 minutes). Adjust seasoning, then turn mixture into a greased 7″ square cake pan. Bake at 375°F 30 minutes. Serve hot or cold.

Savoury potato dish

Potatoes 2 lb
Milk 1 cup
Organic egg 1
Salt ½ tsp
Pepper ¼ tsp
Nutmeg ¼ tsp
Butter or margarine 2 tbsp
Parsley, chopped to garnish

Serves 4

Grease a shallow ovenproof dish large enough to hold the potatoes in a single layer. Dice unpeeled potatoes and spread over base of dish. Beat milk and egg together, add seasoning and nutmeg, and pour over potatoes. Dot with butter and bake, uncovered, about 45 minutes at 400°F until potatoes are tender. Serve immediately, garnished with parsley.

Spiced chickpea croquettes

This generously spiced mixture makes delicious and colorful croquettes, which may be served either hot or cold.

Chickpeas 1 cup
Organic egg 1
Parsley, chopped 3 tbsp
Garlic cloves, crushed 2
Ground cumin 1 tsp
Basil 1 tsp
Salt 1 tsp
Turmeric ½ tsp
Cayenne, pinch

Coating
Beaten egg
Bran

Makes 8 croquettes

Soak chickpeas overnight, then drain. Cook chickpeas in boiling water 1 hour, or until fairly soft. Drain, reserving cooking liquid. Grind or mash peas and mix with 3 tbsp reserved cooking liquid and remaining ingredients. Form mixture into 8 croquettes. Dip in beaten egg and then in bran and deep fry a few minutes, or until golden brown. Drain on paper towels.

"No-cook" rissoles

Mixed nuts ¾ cup
Cottage cheese 1 cup
Parsley, chopped 3 tbsp
Onion, finely chopped 1 tbsp
Salt & pepper to taste
Whole wheat breadcrumbs

Makes 4 rissoles

Coarsely grind nuts. Combine cottage cheese, nuts, parsley, onion, and sufficient salt and pepper to taste. Shape mixture into 4 patties. Coat in breadcrumbs and refrigerate until needed.

Stuffed cabbage leaves

The color and texture of cabbage leaves give this dish an attractive appearance.

Medium-sized green cabbage
  leaves 8
Long-grain brown rice ⅓ cup
Medium-sized onion 1
Oil 2 tbsp
Golden seedless raisins 1 tbsp
Tomato juice ½ cup
Mint, chopped 1 tsp
Salt 1 tsp
Slivered almonds 3 tbsp

Steam cabbage leaves about 5 minutes. Remove coarse central stalk. Boil rice in water 20 minutes, then drain. Chop onion. Heat oil in a saucepan and sauté onion until transparent. Add rice, raisins, and tomato juice and simmer until tomato juice is absorbed. Stir in mint, salt, and almonds. Use rice mixture to fill cabbage leaves, and roll into neat shapes. Place in an ovenproof casserole dish. Dissolve stock cube in water and pour over the cabbage leaves. Cover and bake at

Vegetable stock cube 1
Water ½ cup

Serves 4

350°F about 30 minutes. Serve with baked tomatoes and roast potatoes.

Creamy leek croustade

The delightful contrast in flavors and textures of this layered savoury makes it ideal for a dinner party.

Base
Fresh whole wheat breadcrumbs
   3 cups
Butter or margarine 4 tbsp
Cheddar cheese, grated 1 cup
Mixed nuts, chopped ¾ cup
Mixed herbs ½ tsp
Garlic clove, crushed 1

Sauce
Medium-sized leeks 3
Tomatoes 4
Butter or margarine 4 tbsp
100% whole wheat flour ¼ cup
Milk 1 cup
Salt & pepper to taste
Fresh whole wheat breadcrumbs
   4 tbsp

Serves 6

Put breadcrumbs in a bowl, rub in butter, then add remaining ingredients. Press mixture into a 11 x 7" pan. Bake at 475°F 15-20 minutes, or until golden brown.

Meanwhile, slice leeks and chop tomatoes. Melt butter in a saucepan. Sauté leeks 5 minutes, then stir in flour. Add milk, stirring constantly, then bring to a boil, then reduce heat to a simmer. Add remaining ingredients, except breadcrumbs, and simmer a few minutes to soften tomatoes. Check seasoning. Spoon vegetable mixture over base, sprinkle with breadcrumbs, and heat through in the oven at 350°F 20 minutes. Serve at once.

Spinach roll

Don't be daunted by the preparation and time involved in this recipe. Perseverance is all that is needed to produce this impressive roll.

Medium-sized onion 1
Fresh spinach 2 cups
Butter or margarine 2 tbsp
Parsley, chopped 2 tbsp
Salt & pepper to taste
Ground nutmeg to taste
Organic eggs 4
100% whole wheat flour ½ cup
Cottage cheese 1 cup
Fresh chives or scallions
   chopped 2-3 tbsp

Serves 6

Grease and line a jelly roll pan with waxed paper. Finely chop onion and remove coarse stems from spinach. Melt butter in a saucepan and sauté onion until transparent. Add spinach and cook over high heat, stirring frequently, until no moisture remains. Off the heat, stir in parsley and season generously with salt, pepper, and nutmeg. Turn spinach mixture on to a clean working surface and chop. Let cool (*do not purée the spinach*). Whisk eggs and a pinch of salt

in a bowl until thick and creamy. Fold in cooled spinach and flour carefully, then turn mixture into prepared pan. Level the surface and bake at 400°F 10-12 minutes, or until even and firm to the touch. Turn out on to a piece of waxed paper and roll up like a jelly roll, starting from a short edge and keeping the paper in between the roll. Let cool on a wire tray. Mix cottage cheese with chives. Carefully unroll the roll and spread with cottage cheese. Re-roll and serve.

Stuffed peppers

Medium-sized onion 1
Celery sticks 2
Mushrooms 1 cup
Large tomato 1
Medium-sized carrot 1
Medium-sized rutabaga or
    turnip or parsnip 1
Butter or margarine 2 tbsp
Water ½ cup
Tomato paste 1 tsp
Vegex ½ tsp
Salt & pepper to taste
Medium-sized green or red
    peppers 4
100% whole wheat flour 2 tbsp
Cheddar cheese, grated 1 cup

Serves 4

Chop onion, celery, mushrooms, tomato, and dice carrot and rutabaga. Melt butter and sauté onion, carrot, celery, rutabaga, and mushrooms together 5 minutes. Stir in tomato, water, tomato paste, and Vegex. Cover and simmer 10-15 minutes, or until just tender. Meanwhile, halve peppers lengthwise and remove seeds, then steam 10 minutes. Arrange in an ovenproof serving dish. Drain vegetables, reserving the cooking liquid. Fill peppers with vegetables. Sprinkle flour into vegetable liquid and bring to a boil. Adjust seasoning to taste. Pour over the peppers, sprinkle with cheese, and bake at 400°F 15 minutes. Serve at once.

Cheese, onion & tomato quiche

The classic Cranks cheese quiche—use leeks, mushrooms, zucchini or other vegetables to vary it.

Whole wheat shortcrust pastry
    (see page 181) 8 oz
Medium-sized onion 1
Butter or margarine 2 tbsp
Cheddar cheese, grated 1 cup
Organic eggs 2
Milk ¾ cup
Dijon mustard 1 tsp
Salt & pepper to taste
Large tomato 1

Serves 6

Roll out pastry and use to line a 7½" quiche pan. Chop onion. Melt butter and sauté onion until transparent. Allow to cool slightly, then sprinkle over base of quiche. Sprinkle cheese on top. Beat eggs, milk, mustard, salt, and pepper together and pour into quiche crust. Arrange sliced tomato around the outside edge and bake at 350°F 40-45 minutes, or until set and golden.

Stuffed eggplant

Medium-sized eggplant 2
Large onion 1
Butter or margarine 4 tbsp
Mushrooms 1½ cups
Garlic clove, crushed 1
Parsley, chopped 3 tbsp
Cheddar cheese, grated 1 cup
Salt & pepper to taste

Serves 2-4

Cut eggplant in half lengthwise and scoop out flesh, leaving a ½" shell. Sprinkle shells with salt and leave to one side. Coarsely chop eggplant pulp and chop onion and mushrooms. Melt butter and sauté eggplant and onion until onion is transparent. Add mushrooms and continue cooking a further two minutes. Off the heat, stir in remaining ingredients. Wash and dry eggplant shells. Place in a greased ovenproof dish and spoon in filling. Pour over 4 tbsp water, cover, and bake at 375°F about 45 minutes, or until tender and golden brown.

Homity pies

A good old English country recipe—one of the most popular at Cranks.

Whole wheat shortcrust pastry
   (see page 181) 10 oz.
Medium-sized potatoes 3
Onions 1 lb
Oil 3 tbsp
Butter or margarine 2 tbsp
Parsley, chopped ½ cup
Cheese, grated 1 cup
Garlic cloves, crushed 2
Milk 1 tbsp
Salt & pepper to taste

Makes 6 pies

Roll out pastry and use to line six 4" individual pie pans. Boil or steam potatoes until tender. Chop onions, then sauté in oil until really soft. Combine potatoes and onions, add butter, parsley, 2 oz cheese, garlic, milk, and season well, to taste. Cool, then use to fill pastry shells. Sprinkle with remaining cheese and bake at 425°F 20 minutes, or until golden. Alternatively, use to make one 8" pie. Bake 25-30 minutes.

Crécy plate pie

Served hot or cold, this moist carrot filling complements the crisp texture of the whole wheat pastry.

Medium-sized onions 2 to 3
Medium-sized carrots 3 to 4
Butter or margarine 4 tbsp
Thyme 1 tsp
100% whole wheat flour 2 tbsp
Vegex 1 tsp
Salt & pepper to taste
Whole wheat shortcrust pastry
  (see page 181) 15 oz

Serves 6

Chop onions and grate carrots. Melt butter and sauté onion until transparent. Add carrots and thyme and simmer gently, stirring frequently, 10 minutes. Stir in flour and Vegex and season to taste. Let cool.

Roll out a generous half of the pastry and use to line an 8" pie pan. Fill with vegetable mixture, then top with remaining pastry. Seal edges and flute them. Make two slashes in the center of the pie and bake at 400°F about ½ hour, or until golden. Serve warm or cold.

Crispy mushroom layer

Whole wheat breadcrumbs 2
  cups
Mixed nuts 1 cup
Butter or margarine 8 tbsp
Large onion 1
Mushrooms 2 cups
Medium-sized tomatoes 1 to 2
Salt & pepper to taste
Marjoram 1 tsp

Serves 4-6

Combine breadcrumbs and nuts. Melt 3 oz butter and sauté bread and nut mixture together until golden. Chop onion, mushrooms, and tomatoes, then melt remaining butter and sauté onion until transparent. Add remaining ingredients and simmer gently 5 minutes. In a lightly greased ovenproof dish layer breadcrumbs and vegetables, starting and finishing with a layer of bread and nut mixture. Bake at 375°F ½ hour.

Eggplant & red bean stew

A rich and hearty stew to keep out the winter cold.

WARNING: The red beans must boil vigorously for at least 10 minutes.

Red kidney beans 1⅓ cups
Water 3¾ cups
Large onions 2
Butter or margarine 4 tbsp
Large eggplant 1
Medium-sized tomatoes 1 to 2
Garlic cloves, crushed 2
Tomato paste 2 tbsp

Soak beans overnight. Drain, cover with fresh water, and bring to a boil, making sure that they boil at least 10 minutes; then simmer 45 minutes. Chop onions and tomatoes and dice eggplant. Melt butter and sauté onions until transparent. Add eggplant and continue cooking a further 5 minutes, stirring occasionally. Add beans with their cooking liquid and

Vegetable stock cube 1
Basil 1 tsp
Salt & pepper to taste

Serves 4-6

Mixed root vegetables (onion,
  turnip, carrot, potato),
  chopped 1 cup
Cheddar cheese, grated 1 cup
Sage 1 tsp
Salt ½ tsp
Pepper ¼ tsp
Oil 2 tsp
Whole wheat shortcrust pastry
  (see page 181) 15 oz

Makes 4 turnovers

For the crumble topping
Butter or margarine 8 tbsp
100% whole wheat flour 1½
  cups
Cheddar cheese, grated 1 cup
Mixed nuts, chopped ½ cup

Base
Mixed vegetables (parsnip,
  rutabaga, turnip, potato,
  carrot, etc.) 1½ lb
Large onion 1
Butter or margarine 4 tbsp
100% whole wheat flour ¼ cup
Medium-sized tomatoes 1 to 2
Vegetable stock 1 cup
Milk ½ cup
Parsley, chopped 3 tbsp
Salt & pepper to taste

Serves 6

remaining ingredients. Cover and simmer about 45
minutes, or until beans are tender. Add extra
vegetable stock if needed.

Country turnovers

*Cheese provides protein in these traditional turnovers, which
are ideal for school lunches and picnics.*

Combine the first 6 ingredients in a mixing bowl. Roll
out pastry on a lightly floured surface and cut out
four 7" rounds. Brush edges with water. Spoon filling
into center of each and bring edges up to form a
turnover. Seal edges well. Place on a baking sheet and
bake at 400°F 15 minutes, reduce heat to 325°F and
cook a further 15-20 minutes, or until vegetables are
tender when tested.

Vegetable crumble

*Most people think only of sweet crumbles, but here is an
exciting savoury crumble incorporating cheese, nuts, and
seeds in the topping, covering a mixture of vegetables that
may be varied with the season.*

Rub butter into flour until mixture resembles fine
crumbs. Add cheese, nuts, and sesame seeds.

Chop vegetables, then melt butter in a large saucepan
and sauté onion until transparent. Add prepared
vegetables and cook over gentle heat, stirring
occasionally, 10 minutes. Stir in flour, then add
remaining ingredients. Bring to a boil, reduce heat,
cover, and simmer about 15 minutes, or until
vegetables are just tender. Transfer to an ovenproof
dish. Press crumble topping over vegetables and bake
at 375°F about ½ hour, or until golden.

Cheese & millet croquettes

Millet has quite a bland flavor, which is greatly improved by adding a variety of herbs and other seasonings. Cheese combines particularly well to make these tasty croquettes.

Water 3¾ cups
Mixed herbs ½ tsp
Basil ½ tsp
Cayenne pepper, pinch
Ground bay leaf, pinch
Millet 1¼ cups
Oil 3 tbsp
Medium-sized onion 1
Small pepper (optional) 1
Garlic clove 1
Cheddar cheese, grated 2 cups
Chopped parsley 4 tbsp
Salt & pepper to taste
Beaten egg to coat
Whole wheat breadcrumbs to coat

Makes 8 croquettes

Bring water and herbs to a boil, stir in millet, and simmer gently about 25 minutes, stirring frequently until all the water is absorbed. Heat oil, chop onion, pepper, and garlic, and sauté until onion is transparent. Combine millet, sautéed vegetables, grated cheese, and parsley and season generously with salt and pepper. Let cool, then shape into 8 cakes. Dip in beaten egg and breadcrumbs until evenly coated. Sauté in oil until golden brown. Serve hot or cold.

Leek & cheese quiche

Whole wheat shortcrust pastry
  (see page 181) 10 oz
Large leeks 2
Butter or margarine 2 tbsp
Cayenne, large pinch
Ground nutmeg, large pinch
Organic eggs 3
Milk ½ cup
Sour cream ½ cup
Salt, large pinch
Cheddar cheese, grated 1½ cups

Serves 4-6

Roll out pastry on a lightly floured working surface and use to line a 9" pie pan. Slice leeks and clean thoroughly. Melt butter and sauté leeks until just tender. Season generously with cayenne and nutmeg. Let cool. Whisk eggs, milk, sour cream, and salt together. Sprinkle half the cheese over the base of the pan. Spread leeks on top and sprinkle with remaining cheese. Pour egg custard into pan. Bake at 400°F about ½ hour, or until risen and golden. Serve warm or cold.

PUDDINGS & DESSERTS

Many will undoubtedly say that a dessert at the end of a meal is as unnecessary as a starter at the beginning. Certainly most health-conscious people will settle for a simple form of fruit or yogurt to complete a meal. Cranks, not wanting to go too far down the road of puritanism, prefers to subscribe to the view that "a little of what you fancy does you good."

Just for a moment, consider your favorite dessert recipe and then imagine it transformed with all the goodness of natural whole food ingredients—cream, organic eggs, raw sugar, 100% whole wheat flour—and you have Cranks daily fare!

Creamy yogurt pie

The combination of natural yogurt and soft cheeses gives this pie a delicate flavor. Make the plain one first, then try the variations.

Whole wheat shortcrust pastry
  (see page 181) 6 oz
Skim milk powder ½ cup
Ricotta cheese ¾ cup
Cream cheese ¾ cup
Natural yogurt ½ cup
Honey 3 tbsp
Ground nutmeg or cinnamon

Serves 4-6

Roll out pastry and use to line an 8″ fluted pie pan. Bake the weighted shell at 400°F 15 minutes. Meanwhile, blend together milk powder, ricotta and cream cheese, natural yogurt, and honey until smooth. Pour blended mixture into warm pastry, sprinkle with ground spices, and return to the oven for 15 minutes. Allow to cool in pan, then refrigerate until set.

VARIATIONS
Citrus pie Pare the rind from 1 lemon, cut away all the white pith, then coarsely chop the flesh, removing any seeds. Add rind and lemon flesh to the ingredients and blend together in a blender until smooth. *Omit spices.* Decorate with half slices of lemon.

Cinnamon pie Stir ⅓ cup golden seedless raisins and 1 tsp ground cinnamon into blended mixture.

Sunshine pie Repeat as for CITRUS PIE above, but substitute 1 small orange for lemon. Decorate with half slices of orange.

Banana yogurt pie

Cooked banana has a natural sweetness and distinctive flavor to contrast with the sharpness of natural yogurt and orange.

Whole wheat shortcrust pastry
  (see page 181) 6 oz
Bananas 6
Natural yogurt ½ cup
Orange, grated rind of ½

Serves 4-6

Roll out pastry and use to line an 8″ fluted pie pan. Mash bananas and beat in 4 tbsp yogurt. Pour banana mixture into pie shell. Spoon remaining yogurt over the filling and, using a knife, swirl yogurt through the mixture to give a decorative effect. Sprinkle with orange rind. Bake at 400°F 25-30 minutes. Cool in pan and chill. Serve cold.

Puréed fruit gelatin

Bananas 2
Dessert apple 1
Pitted dates ½ cup
Apple juice, freshly extracted or
    bottled (see page 192)
Agar-agar 2 tsp

Serves 4-6

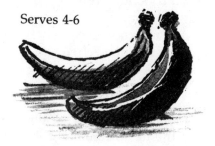

Coarsely chop fruit. Put bananas, apples, and dates into a blender with ½ cup apple juice. Blend until smooth. Make up to 2 cups with more apple juice. Place purée in a saucepan, whisk in agar-agar, and cook over a gentle heat, stirring all the time until agar-agar is dissolved. Bring to a boil. Pour into 2 cup mold or individual dishes. Refrigerate until needed. If wished, decorate with fresh whipped cream or sour cream.

Lemon cheesecake

For the base
Whole wheat dessert crackers or
    graham crackers 1 cup
Butter or margarine, melted 4
    tbsp

For the filling
Lemons 2
Raw sugar ⅔ cup
Cream cheese 1½ cups
Ricotta cheese 1½ cups
Heavy cream ½ cup

Whipped cream, green grapes,
    or grated lemon rind to
    decorate

Serves 6-8

This cheesecake is neither baked nor set with gelatin. It relies on the weight of the ingredients to hold its shape, so chill well and handle with care.

Finely crush crackers and stir into butter. Press mixture into base of an 8″ springform cake pan.

Grate rind from lemons and squeeze out juice. Place in a bowl with sugar. Beat well. Slowly beat in cheeses and continue beating until mixture is smooth. Whip cream until it holds its shape and fold in cheese. Spread cheese mixture over base and level surface. Cover and refrigerate several hours.

Turn cheesecake out on to a serving plate. Decorate with whipped cream and grape halves or lemon rind.

Lemon meringue pie

Whole wheat shortcrust pastry
    (see page 181) 6 oz
Lemons, grated rind & juice of 2
Water ½ cup
Crystallized honey ⅓ cup

A family favorite in a new guise.

Roll out pastry and use to line an 8″ pie pan. Bake the weighted shell at 425°F about 15 minutes. In a saucepan mix together lemon rind and juice, water, honey, and cornmeal.

Cornmeal 3 tbsp
Organic eggs, separated 2
Raw sugar ½ cup

Serves 6

Bring to a boil, stirring, and cook until thickened. Off the heat, beat in egg yolks. Allow to cool before spooning into pastry shell. Stiffly whisk egg whites until they stand in peaks. Whisk in sugar a spoonful at a time until stiff. Spoon onto lemon filling and bake at 325°F about 20 minutes, or until golden. Let cool before cutting.

Sticky prune cake

Prunes 1 cup
Raw sugar ⅔ cup
Vegetable oil ½ cup
Organic eggs 2
100% whole wheat flour 1¼ cups
Baking soda ½ tsp
Ground cinnamon 1 tsp
Allspice ½ tsp
Ground nutmeg ½ tsp
Ground cloves, pinch
Buttermilk ½ cup

Topping
Raw sugar ⅓ cup
Buttermilk 3 tbsp
Molasses or honey 1 tbsp
Vanilla extract few drops

Serves 6-8

Wash prunes and place in a saucepan. Just cover with water and bring to a boil. Simmer 10-15 minutes, or until just tender. Drain, remove pits and roughly chop. In a bowl, whisk together sugar, oil, and eggs until thick and smooth. Stir in flour, baking soda, and spices. Beat well. Stir in prunes and buttermilk. Pour mixture into a greased and lined 9″ layer cake pan, and bake at 350°F about 30 minutes, or until firm to the touch.

Warm ingredients for topping together in a small saucepan. Prick cake all over with a skewer and spoon syrup over the top. Let cool in the pan. Cut in wedges. Serve with fresh or sour cream.

Raw sugar jam tart

Whole wheat shortcrust pastry
 (*see page 181*) 6 oz
Raw sugar jam 8 tbsp

Serves 6

Roll out a generous two-thirds of the pastry and use to line an 8″ pie pan. Spread the jam over the base. Roll out remaining pastry and cut into ½″ strips. Arrange in a lattice over jam, pressing ends of strips

to secure them. Neaten edges of tart with prongs of a fork. Bake at 400°F 20-25 minutes, or until pastry is golden.

Baked egg custard

An unusual variation of the traditional egg custard.

Whisk together eggs and milk, then stir in remaining ingredients, except raisins. Grease a shallow 2 pt ovenproof dish with butter or margarine. Sprinkle raisins over the base and pour egg custard into dish. Place dish in a deep baking pan and pour in water to within 1" of the top. Bake at 350°F about 1 hour, or until just set. Serve warm or cold.

Organic eggs 4
Milk 2¼ cups
Cashew nuts, finely ground ¼ cup
Raw sugar 2 tbsp
Vanilla extract 1 tsp
Grated orange rind ½ tsp
Ground nutmeg ¼ tsp
Raisins ⅓ cup

Serves 4-6

Orange & banana trifle

Heat milk and sugar in a saucepan to just below boiling. Beat eggs, vanilla extract, and cornstarch together in a bowl, then whisk in milk. Return custard to saucepan and cook over very gentle heat, stirring continuously until custard thickens enough to coat the back of a wooden spoon. Remove from heat at once.

Milk 2¼ cups
Raw sugar 2 tbsp
Organic eggs 4
Vanilla extract ½ tsp
Cornstarch 1 tbsp
Left-over sponge cake ¾ lb
Oranges 3
Bananas, peeled and sliced 2
Fresh cream, whipped 1 cup
Slivered almonds, toasted 3 tbsp

Serves 8

Slice sponge cake and place in the base of a serving dish. Remove skin and white pith from oranges and chop them, reserving the juice. Spoon juice over the sponge, then arrange oranges and bananas on top. Pour warm custard over fruit, cover, and refrigerate until needed. Decorate with whipped cream and slivered almonds before serving.

Creamy bran & apple chunks

This is so quick to make, yet tastes delicious.

Finely chop apples. Mix sour cream and milk together in a bowl. Stir in remaining ingredients and transfer

Small dessert apples 2
Sour cream ½ cup
Milk 2 tbsp

Walnuts, chopped 3 tbsp
Honey 1-2 tbsp
Bran 3 tbsp
Apple slices 8

Serves 4

to individual serving dishes. Decorate with apple slices.

If this dessert is kept in the refrigerator for several days it will tend to thicken. Thin to the required consistency with a little milk.

VARIATIONS
Carob and apple Omit walnuts and add 3 tbsp carob powder.

Orange and nut Substitute 2 small peeled oranges or mandarins for apples, and add a little grated orange or lemon rind.

Apple pie

Cooking apples 2 lb
Water 1 tbsp
Raw sugar 4 tbsp
Lemon, grated rind of ½
Ground cloves ¼ tsp
Whole wheat shortcrust pastry
   (see page 181) 15 oz

Serves 6

Wipe, core, and slice apples, then place apples, water, sugar, lemon rind, and cloves in a saucepan. Simmer 10 minutes, stirring occasionally. Do not allow apple to become mushy. Let cool.

Roll out pastry and use a generous half to line a 9″ pie pan. Fill with apple. Use remaining pastry as a top crust. Seal edges well, make a hole in the center, then flute to give a decorative edge. Bake at 400°F about 25 minutes, or until golden. Serve warm or cold.

Bakewell tart

An old English classic in the Cranks style.

Whole wheat shortcrust pastry
  (see page 181) 6 oz
Jam 4 tbsp
Raw sugar ½ cup
Butter or margarine 6 tbsp
Organic eggs, beaten 2
Almond extract ½ tsp
Soy flour ½ cup
Baking powder ½ tsp
Slivered almonds 3 tbsp

Serves 4-6

Roll out pastry and use it to line an 8" pie pan. Spread base with jam. Cream sugar and butter together until light and fluffy. Beat in eggs a little at a time (if necessary add some soy flour to prevent curdling). Beat in almond extract, soy flour, and baking powder. Spread mixture carefully over the jam. Sprinkle slivered almonds on top and bake at 325°F about 1 hour, or until risen and golden.

Spiced bread pudding

A clever way to use stale bread to make a lovely pudding.

Stale whole wheat bread 8 slices
Milk 1 cup
Currants, golden seedless raisins
  & raisins, mixed ⅔ cup
Butter or margarine 4 tbsp,
  grated
Raw sugar ⅔ cup
Allspice 1 tbsp
Organic egg 1
Milk 4 tbsp
Ground nutmeg, pinch

Serves 6

Roughly break up the bread and place in a mixing bowl with milk. Let soak. Add dried fruits, butter, sugar, and allspice. Beat well. Whisk together egg and milk and add to bread mixture. Turn into a greased shallow ovenproof dish, level the surface, and sprinkle with ground nutmeg. Bake at 350°F about 45 minutes, or until set. Serve hot or cold.

Tangy apple swirl

Cooking apples 1 lb
Butter or margarine 2 tbsp
Raw sugar ⅓ cup
Ground cloves, pinch
Lemon, grated rind of ½
Natural yogurt 1 cup

Serves 4

Peel, core, and chop apples. Place all the ingredients, except yogurt, in a saucepan. Cook over gentle heat, stirring occasionally until the apples are soft. Stir thoroughly to give a rough purée. Let cool. In a glass serving dish, or individual dishes, spoon alternate spoons of yogurt and apple until it is all used up. With a knife, swirl mixtures to give a decorative effect. Serve chilled.

Grape & banana pie

A special occasion pie with a rich pastry base.

Pastry
100% whole wheat flour 1 cup
Egg yolks 2
Butter or margarine, softened 4
    tbsp
Raw sugar ⅓ cup

Filling
Egg yolks 2
100% whole wheat flour ¼ cup
Cornmeal 2 tbsp
Raw sugar 2 tbsp
Milk 1 cup
Lemon, grated rind of ½

Topping
Banana 1
Lemon, juice of ½
Black grapes, halved & seeds
    removed ⅔ cup
Apricot jam 2 tbsp

Serves 6

For the pastry
Put flour in a bowl, and make a well in the center.
Put egg yolks, butter, and sugar in the center and
work together, drawing flour in with the fingertips, to
give a soft, manageable dough. Roll out on a lightly
floured surface and use to line a 7½″ fluted pie pan.
Prick base, chill ½ hour, then bake weighted shell at
375°F about 20 minutes. Let cool. Remove from pan.

For the filling
Put egg yolks, flour, cornmeal, sugar, and a little milk
into a bowl and mix to a smooth paste. Heat milk,
then pour over the egg mixture, stirring all the time.
Return to pan and cook over gentle heat, stirring until
thickened. Off the heat, stir in lemon rind. Cover and
let cool. Spread over the base of the pie shell.

For the topping
Peel and slice banana, dip in lemon juice, drain,
reserving juice. Arrange a circle of grape halves, then
one of banana slices on top of the pie. Repeat until
fruit is used up. Mix apricot jam and lemon juice in a
saucepan. Heat gently, then brush over fruit to glaze.
Chill until needed.

ALTERNATIVE
Strawberry pie Use ½ lb strawberries and 2 tbsp
strawberry jam for the glaze.

Junket

*Served with stewed fruit, this is an ideal dessert for all the
family, although it has been regarded as an invalid delicacy
in the past.*

Fresh milk 2¼ cups
Raw sugar 1 tsp
Vegetarian rennet 1 tsp
Ground nutmeg

Serves 4

Heat milk and sugar in a saucepan to 110°F. Off the
heat, stir in rennet. Pour milk into a serving dish.
Sprinkle with nutmeg and let cool.

If you do not have a thermometer, test milk with the
tip of a finger. The milk should feel comfortably hot.

Toffeed rhubarb fool

Rhubarb 1 lb
Raw sugar ⅓ cup
Butter or margarine 4 tbsp
Heavy cream 1 cup

Serves 4-6

Trim and slice rhubarb, then put rhubarb, sugar and butter in a saucepan over gentle heat until butter melts. Simmer gently until rhubarb is soft and thick, stirring occasionally. Chill until cold. Whip cream until it holds its shape, then fold in rhubarb. Spoon into individual glass dishes. Serve chilled.

Custard tart

Whole wheat shortcrust pastry
(see page 181) 9 oz
Organic eggs 2
Milk 1 cup
Raw sugar 1 tbsp
Ground nutmeg

Serves 4-6

Roll out pastry and use it to line a 7" pie pan. Whisk together eggs, milk, and sugar and pour into pastry. Sprinkle generously with ground nutmeg and bake at 375°F about 25 minutes, or until lightly set. Let cool in the pan.

Walnut pie

Deliciously rich and sticky, this rather expensive recipe can be kept for a special treat.

Whole wheat shortcrust pastry
(see page 181) 15 oz
Shelled walnuts, coarsely
   chopped 1⅔ cups
Heavy cream ½ cups
Honey ½ cup
Organic eggs 3
Raw sugar ⅔ cup

Serves 6

Roll out a generous half of the pastry and use it to line a 9½" pie pan. Sprinkle walnuts over base. Whisk together remaining ingredients and pour carefully over walnuts. Roll out remaining pastry and use as top crust. Seal well at edges. Bake at 400°F 15 minutes, reduce heat to 350°F and cook a further 25 minutes. Leave until cold before cutting. Serve with fresh or sour cream.

Hazelnut & black cherry tart

100% whole wheat flour ¾ cup
Ground cinnamon ½ tsp
Raw sugar ½ cup
Hazelnuts, finely ground ¼ cup
Lemon, grated rind of ½
Unsalted butter 4 oz
Egg yolks 2
Vanilla extract ¼ tsp
Black cherry jam 1½ cups
Beaten egg 1 tbsp
Sour cream 1 tbsp

Serves 6

In a bowl, combine the first 5 ingredients. Rub in butter until mixture resembles breadcrumbs. Add egg yolks and vanilla extract and work together to give a soft dough. Wrap in plastic wrap or waxed paper and chill at least 30 minutes. On a lightly floured surface, roll out three-quarters of pastry and use to line an 8" springform pan. (The pastry may crack a little; if it does, simply press it into the pan.) Spread jam over the base of the pastry. Use remaining pastry to make strips for the top of the tart. Lay them across the top of the jam in a lattice effect. Neaten edges. Beat together beaten egg and sour cream and carefully brush pastry with it. Bake at 350°F about 40 minutes until crisp and golden on top. Let cool completely before removing from pan and serving.

Carrageenan citrus gelatin

Carrageenan has a unique flavor that permeates this dessert and gives it a dark opaque look.

Water 2¼ cups
Carrageenan 1 oz
Lemons 2
Orange 1
Raw sugar ⅔ cup
Green grapes to decorate

Serves 4

Put water and carrageenan in a saucepan. Pare rind from lemons and orange and add it to pan. Bring to a boil, then simmer 15 minutes. Squeeze juice from fruits. Add to hot liquid. Put sugar in a bowl and strain hot liquid over sugar, stirring until it dissolves. Pour into a serving dish and leave until set. Decorate with grape halves.

Devon apple cake

This traditional Devon recipe, first introduced into Cranks restaurant at Dartington in Devon, should of course always be served with whipped cream!

100% whole wheat flour 2 cups
3 tsp baking powder
Salt ¼ tsp
Ground cinnamon 1 tsp
Allspice 1 tsp

Grease and flour base of a 7½" square cake pan. In a bowl combine flour, baking powder, salt, cinnamon, allspice, and sugar. Rub in butter or margarine until mixture resembles fine crumbs. Wash, core, and

Raw sugar ⅔ cup
Butter or margarine 4 oz
Cooking apples 2 cups
Organic egg, beaten 1

Serves about 6

coarsely chop apples, then add apples and beaten egg to mixture and stir quickly to combine. Spread evenly in pan and bake at 375°F about ½ hour, or until risen and firm to the touch. Allow to cool in pan before cutting into squares.

Carob blancmange

An old favorite, using carob instead of chocolate powder.

Carob powder 3 tbsp
Raw sugar 3 tbsp
Unflavored gelatin 1 tbsp
Water 3 tbsp
Milk 2 cups
Whipped cream to decorate
Carob bar to decorate

Serves 4-6

In a bowl, mix together carob powder, sugar, gelatin, and cold water to a smooth paste. Heat milk to just below boiling and pour over carob paste, stirring all the time. Return to saucepan and simmer 2 minutes, stirring continuously. Pour into a wet 1 pt mold. Chill until set. Unmold and decorate with whipped cream and grated carob bar.

Brandied prune mousse

Prunes 1¾ cups
Brandy 1 tbsp
Heavy cream ½ cup
Egg whites 2

Serves 6

Cover prunes with water and allow to soak overnight. Bring to a boil, reduce heat, cover, and simmer about 15 minutes, or until really soft. Drain, reserving juice, and let cool. Discard pits and blend prunes in a blender, using about 4 tbsp of reserved juice, until prunes are a thick purée. Stir in brandy. Whip cream until it just holds its shape. Stiffly whisk egg whites. Fold whipped cream and then egg whites into prune purée. Spoon into a serving dish or individual dishes. Cover and chill until needed.

Buttermilk dessert

This dessert has an intriguing flavor and texture to keep friends guessing!

Pumpernickel bread, grated 4
  cups
Buttermilk 2 cups
Lemon, grated rind of 1
Crystallized honey 3 tbsp
Raisins ⅓ cup
Vanilla extract 1 tsp

Serves 6

Mix all ingredients together. Cover and chill until needed. Serve in individual glass dishes.

This mixture will thicken on standing. Thin with extra buttermilk, as needed.

Honey & apple tart

Medium-sized cooking apples 2
Honey ½ cup
Lemon, juice & rind of 1
Fresh whole wheat breadcrumbs
  3 cups
Whole wheat shortcrust pastry
  (see page 181) 9 oz

Serves 4-6

Grate apples and mix together with honey, lemon rind and juice, and breadcrumbs. Roll out pastry on a lightly floured surface and use to line an 8" pie pan. Spoon filling in center, level surface, and bake at 400°F 30-35 minutes, or until firm to the touch. Serve warm or cold.

Date & apple squares

Cooking apples 1 lb
Shelled walnuts ½ cup
Pitted dates 1 cup
100% whole wheat flour 1 cup
1½ tsp baking powder
Raw sugar ⅔ cup
Honey 1 tbsp
Butter or margarine, melted 1 oz
Organic egg 1
Salt, pinch

Serves 4-6

Dice apples, chop walnuts and dates, and place in a bowl with all the remaining ingredients. Mix well to combine evenly, then spread mixture into a lightly greased 8" square cake pan. Bake at 400°F about ½ hour, or until golden and risen. Cut into squares and serve warm with fresh or sour cream.

Molasses tart

Molasses ½ cup
Honey ½ cup
Lemon, grated rind of ½
Dried coconut 1 cup
Fresh whole wheat breadcrumbs
   1½ cups
Whole wheat shortcrust pastry
   (see page 181) 9 oz

Serves 6

Combine the first 5 ingredients and stir well until evenly mixed. On a lightly floured surface roll out pastry and use it to line an 8" pie pan. Pour filling in center and bake at 400°F 30-35 minutes, or until pastry is golden. Let cool in pan. Serve with ice cream or sour cream.

Apple crumble

Cooking apples 1½ lb
Water 3 tbsp
Raw sugar ⅔ cup
Allspice 1 tsp

For the crumble
Butter or margarine 3 oz
100% whole wheat flour 1½ cups

Serves 4

Wipe, core, and slice apples, then place apples, water, half the sugar, and allspice in a saucepan and simmer gently about 10 minutes. Do not allow apples to become too soft. Place apple mixture in a 2 pt ovenproof dish. Let cool.

Rub butter into flour until mixture resembles fine crumbs. Stir in remaining sugar. Press crumble topping onto apples. Bake at 400°F 20-25 minutes. Serve warm.

Bread & butter pudding

Thin slices of whole wheat bread
   4
Butter or margarine 2 tbsp
Raw sugar 1 tbsp
Mixed raisins & currants ⅓ cup
Milk 2 cups
Organic eggs 2
Ground cinnamon ¼ tsp
Nutmeg ¼ tsp

Serves 4

Cut 4 thin slices of whole wheat bread, preferably stale. Spread bread with butter or margarine, and cut each piece into quarters. Arrange half of the bread, buttered side up, on the base of a 1½ pt ovenproof dish. Sprinkle with half the sugar and dried fruit. Repeat layer once more. Whisk together milk, eggs, and spices. Pour custard over bread. Bake at 350°F about 45 minutes, or until just set. Serve hot.

Baked apples

A recipe often overlooked. Choose best quality apples for good results.

Medium-sized cooking apples 4
Raw sugar 2 tbsp
Raisins ⅓ cup
Whole cloves 8
Butter or margarine 2 tbsp
Honey 2 tbsp
Water 2 tbsp

Serves 4

Wipe and core apples. Score a line around the center of each. Place in an ovenproof dish, allowing a little space between each. Combine sugar and raisins and use to fill center. Press 2 cloves into center of each apple, and dot with butter. Spoon honey, then water, over apples. Bake at 400°F 30-45 minutes, or until tender. Serve with fresh or sour cream or with EGG CUSTARD *(see page 122).*

Pouding Alsace

A superior version of Eve's pudding, with a delicious flavor and light texture.

Cooking apples 1 lb
Butter or margarine 6 tbsp
Apricot jam ¼ cup
Raw sugar ½ cup
Organic eggs, separated 3
Fresh whole wheat breadcrumbs
    1 cup
100% whole wheat flour 2 tbsp
Cinnamon 1 tsp

Serves 6

Core and slice apples. Melt 2 tbsp butter in a saucepan, add apples, and cook over low heat about 5 minutes. Do not allow them to get mushy. Off the heat, stir in jam and turn mixture into a greased ovenproof serving dish. Cream remaining butter and sugar together until light and fluffy. Beat in egg yolks. Combine breadcrumbs, flour, and cinnamon. Stiffly whisk egg whites. Fold dry ingredients, then egg whites, into creamed mixture. Spoon over apples and level surface. Bake at 325°F about 40 minutes, or until sponge is set and golden.

Mincemeat & apple 'jalousie'

A very special dessert, with an exciting filling—it was first tried out in Cranks in Dartington where we discovered that whipped cream is a must with it, especially when making the dessert for a special occasion.

Cooking apples 1¼ cups
Whole wheat shortcrust pastry
    (see page 181) 1 recipe

Wash, core, and coarsely chop apples. Add 1 tbsp water and cook over low heat about 10 minutes, or until just soft. Cool. Roll out pastry on a lightly

continued

Mincemeat 1 cup
Beaten egg to glaze
Slivered almonds 3 tbsp
Honey 2 tbsp

Serves 4-6

floured surface to an oblong 18 x 7″. Trim edges and cut in half to give two oblongs 9 x 7″. Flour one oblong lightly and fold in half lengthwise. Using a sharp knife, cut a series of slits through the pastry about ½″ apart, and to within 1″ of edges. Unfold.

Put plain oblong of pastry on a greased baking sheet and spread mincemeat down the center. Spoon apple down both sides of mincemeat to within 1″ of edge. Dampen edges of pastry and carefully place second piece of pastry on top. Seal edges well, then flute to give a decorative edge. Brush with beaten egg, sprinkle with slivered almonds, and bake at 425°F 20-25 minutes, or until golden. While still warm, brush with honey. Serve warm or cold.

Home-made yogurt

Making yogurt at home is very easy and fun, too. Buy a container of natural yogurt to begin with, but once you have made a batch of yogurt, keep a tablespoon to use as a "starter" for the next batch.

Fresh milk is the most popular base, but yogurt can be made entirely from reconstituted skim milk—which cuts down on calories for those trying to watch their weight. Follow the instructions on the can for reconstituting the powder, then proceed as with fresh milk.

Natural yogurt may be served on its own, with fresh or stewed fruit, or honey, stirred into soups and stews, and used in baking.

Chopped or puréed fruits, raw sugar jams, grated carob or savoury flavorings, such as tomato juice, finely chopped herbs, and grated vegetables, may be added to natural yogurt.

Fresh cow or goat milk 2¼ cups
Natural yogurt 1 tbsp
Skim milk powder (optional) 1-2
   tbsp

Serves 4

Preheat a heatproof dish with a well-fitting lid, or thermos flask, with boiling water. Heat milk to body temperature: 98°F. Put yogurt into a bowl and stir in milk powder, if used. Pour a little of warm milk on to

yogurt, stir well, then pour yogurt into pan of milk. Stir well again, then pour into warmed dish and cover with lid. Cover container with a thick cloth and leave in a warm place, such as on the back of the stove, overnight, or until milk clots.

If a thermos flask is used, it is, of course, not necessary to leave it in a warm place, so this is probably the most convenient method.

Christmas pudding

A rich, dark and fruity pudding–made every year at Cranks Dartington Branch and sold in all the Cranks shops.

Whole wheat breadcrumbs 1½ cups
100% whole wheat flour ¾ cup
Currants 1⅓ cups
Raisins 1⅓ cups
Golden seedless raisins 1⅓ cups
Almonds, chopped 3 tbsp
Raw sugar 1⅓ cups
Ground allspice ½ tsp
Ground nutmeg ¼ tsp
Butter or margarine 6 oz
Organic eggs 3
Raw sugar marmalade 1 tbsp
Sherry ½ cup
Lemon, grated rind of ½

Makes two 1¾ lb puddings

Thoroughly combine all dry ingredients together in a large mixing bowl. Melt butter or margarine, beat eggs, and add all remaining ingredients to bowl. Stir well until evenly mixed. Grease 2 pudding molds and press mixture into them. Cut 2 circles of waxed paper –about 4" larger than the tops of pudding molds– brush them with oil and make a pleat in each. Place over molds and secure with string. Top with a piece of aluminum foil. Steam 6 hours. Reheat by steaming a further 1½ hours. Serve with fresh cream or a sweet sauce.

CAKES & SCONES

It is very difficult to believe that Marie Antoinette, who must have been a reasonably intelligent woman, even though spoiled and over-privileged, can have made such a stupid remark as "Well, let them eat cake" when told that the population of Paris was starving for the want of sufficient bread! But the story does highlight the position of cake as a luxury food, which it undoubtedly is.

So let us accept that we don't *need* cake, but that it can nevertheless be a very pleasant addition to a social tea time–and while we are about it, let us at lease rob the occasion of the worst horrors of fattening and de-nourishing white flour, white sugar, and chemically flavored and colored jams.

Again, there is a prejudice in the public mind that 100% whole wheat means heavy. This is pure fallacy, and a visit to any Cranks to experience a piece of delicious light whole wheat sponge cake will prove the point.

Cake making needs to take place without hurry. All the ingredients should be taken out of the refrigerator long before starting so that they come up to room temperature. Each ingredient should then be carefully mixed and beaten into the mixture before adding the next. The more you enjoy making the cake the better the cake will be!

Belgian cake

This unusual cake with a surprisingly light texture is an ideal way to disguise left-over mincemeat in the New Year.

Butter or margarine 8 tbsp
Raw sugar ½ cup
Organic eggs, beaten 2
100% whole wheat flour 1¼ cups
1¾ tsp baking powder
Raw sugar mincemeat 1 cup
Water 1 tbsp

Cream butter and sugar together until pale and fluffy. Beat in eggs a little at a time. Fold in flour and baking powder, then fold in mincemeat and water. Spoon mixture into a greased and floured 8" square cake pan. Level surface. Bake at 325°F about 30 minutes, or until well risen and golden. Cool in pan.

Old-fashioned ginger cake

100% whole wheat flour 2 cups
3 tsp baking powder
Baking soda ½ tsp
Ground ginger 2 tsp
Butter or margarine 4 oz
Raw sugar 1 cup
Molasses 4 tbsp
Milk 2 tbsp
Organic egg 1

Stir together flour, baking soda, baking powder, and ginger. Melt butter in a saucepan with sugar and molasses. Cool slightly, then beat in milk and egg. Stir liquid ingredients into flour. Beat well, then turn into a greased and floured loaf pan. Bake at 350°F 40-45 minutes, until risen and firm to the touch. Cool on a wire rack.

100% Whole wheat sponge

The Cranks version of a whisked sponge recipe in which a high proportion of eggs to flour and sugar gives it a special texture.

Organic eggs 4
Vanilla extract ½ tsp
Raw sugar 2 tbsp
100% whole wheat flour ¼ cup
Raw sugar jam or whipped cream to fill

Line two 7" layer pans with parchment paper. Put eggs, vanilla extract and sugar in a bowl and whisk until really thick. Fold in flour with a metal spoon or spatula. Divide mixture between pans, level surface, and bake at 350°F 15-20 minutes, or until golden and firm to the touch. Cool slightly in the pan before transferring to a wire rack. When cold, sandwich together with jam and/or whipped cream. For special occasions, top with BROWN SUGAR ICING (*see page 139*).

Jelly roll

Organic eggs 4
Vanilla extract ½ tsp
Raw sugar 2 tbsp
100% whole wheat flour ¼ cup
Raw sugar jam 6 tbsp
Heavy cream, whipped ½ cup

Line a 7½ x 11½" jelly roll pan with parchment paper. Put eggs, vanilla extract, and sugar in bowl and whisk together until really thick–this will take 10-25 minutes, depending on whether you use an electric mixer or a whisk. Fold in flour and pour mixture into prepared pan and level surface. Bake at 350°F about 20 minutes, or until golden brown and firm to the touch. Turn out carefully onto a piece of waxed paper. Remove the lining paper from the cooked jelly roll and, with a sharp knife, make an indentation about ½" from one short edge. Starting at that edge, roll sponge with paper in between and let cool. When cool, unroll and spread with jam and cream, then re-roll.

Christmas cake

A rich fruit cake that improves with keeping. This recipe can also be used for a wedding, birthday, or other celebration cake.

Raisins 6⅔ cups
Currants 3 cups
Pitted dates, chopped 1¼ cups
Cooked prunes, pitted & chopped ⅔ cup
Slivered almonds 1⅔ cups
Butter or margarine 14 oz
Raw sugar 2⅓ cups
Organic eggs 8
Lemon, grated rind of 1
Orange, grated rind of 1
Molasses 1 tbsp
100% whole wheat flour 4 cups
Salt 1 tsp

Grease and line a cake pan with a double thickness of parchment paper. Secure brown paper around the outside of the pan. Combine raisins, currants, dates, prunes, and almonds in a large bowl. Cream butter and sugar until pale and fluffy, then beat in eggs one at a time. Stir in lemon and orange rind and molasses. If there is any sign of curdling, stir in a spoonful of flour. Combine flour, salt, and spices and fold into mixture alternately with mixed fruits. Stir in sherry. Turn mixture into prepared pan. Smooth surface and bake at 300°F 1 hour. Reduce heat to 275°F for a further 4 hours. Cover with waxed paper if surface is

Ground nutmeg, allspice,
cinnamon & ginger 1 tsp *each*
Sherry 5 tbsp

Makes 10" round or 9" square
cake

overbrowning. Let cake cool in its pan overnight, then remove from pan and wrap in a double thickness of aluminum foil. Store in a cool dry place until needed.

To decorate
Cover with 2 lb almond paste or mock marzipan and icing *(see following three recipes).*

Almond paste

Ground almonds 1 cup
Raw sugar ⅔ cup
Beaten egg 2 tbsp
Almond extract ½ tsp

Makes about ½ lb

Sift ground almonds and sugar into a bowl. Stir together egg and almond extract and mix with almonds to form a soft, manageable dough.

Mock marzipan

An alternative to almond paste for vegans.

Raw sugar 1⅔ cups
Soy flour 1 cup
Margarine, softened 2 oz
Almond extract 1 tsp
Water 1-2 tbsp

Makes about 1 lb

Mix dry ingredients together in a bowl and rub in margarine. Add almond extract and enough water to mix to a soft, manageable dough.

Raw sugar icing

Raw sugar ⅔ cup
Lemon juice 2 tbsp
Vanilla extract, few drops

Mill sugar in a coffee grinder or pass through a fine sieve. Add lemon juice and vanilla extract and beat until smooth. Use to coat cookies or the top of a cake.

Luscious lemon cake

A warm syrup is poured over the finished cake to give it an extra lemony flavor—quite irresistible!

Butter or margarine 8 tbsp
Raw sugar ¾ cup
Lemon, grated rind & juice of 1
Organic egg 1
100% whole wheat flour 1 cup
1½ tsp baking powder

Grease and flour the base of a 7" square cake pan. Heat butter and sugar over low heat until melted. Off the heat, stir in lemon rind. Whisk egg in a bowl, and then whisk it into sugar mixture. Fold in flour and baking powder, and turn mixture into prepared pan. Bake at 350°F about 30 minutes, or until just firm to the touch. Warm remaining 1 oz sugar with lemon juice. Prick cake all over with a fork or toothpick and spoon syrup over cake. Leave in pan to cool. Cut into squares.

Carob cake

This cake just had to be included because of the continuing requests for the recipe from our customers.

Butter or margarine 4 oz
Raw sugar ⅔ cup
Organic eggs, separated 4
Vanilla extract ½ tsp
Almond extract ½ tsp
Carob powder ½ cup
100% whole wheat flour ⅓ cup
Ground almonds ½ cup

Filling
Pitted prunes ½ cup
Apricot jam 2 tbsp

Topping
Water 2 tbsp
Carob bar 2.8 oz
Butter or margarine 1 oz
Slivered almonds to decorate

Grease and flour the base of two 7" cake pans. Cream butter and sugar until light and fluffy. Beat in egg yolks and extracts. Combine carob powder, flour, and ground almonds. Stiffly whisk egg whites. Fold dry ingredients and egg whites alternately into mixture. Spoon mixture into prepared pans and level surface. Bake at 350°F about 20 minutes, or until just firm to the touch. Cool on a wire rack.

For the filling Place prunes in a saucepan, barely cover with water, and simmer until tender. Drain, allow to cool, then remove pits and coarsely chop prunes. Spread apricot jam on one of the cakes, top with prunes, then sandwich the two cakes together.

For the topping Place water and broken carob bar in a saucepan over low heat, and stir until carob is melted. Take off the heat and beat in butter. Allow to cool slightly, then spread over the top of the cake. Decorate with a ring of slivered almonds round the edge.

Date & coconut gâteau

Butter or margarine 8 tbsp
Raw sugar ⅔ cup
Organic eggs 2
100% whole wheat flour ¾ cup
1 tsp baking powder
Dried coconut ⅓ cup

Filling
Pitted dates, chopped ¾ cup
Water 3 tbsp
Egg yolks 2
Raw sugar 2 tbsp
Milk 2 tbsp
Cornstarch 1½ tsp
Butter or margarine 2 oz

Topping
Dried coconut, toasted ⅔ cup
Whole dates 4
Honey to glaze

Grease and flour the base of two 7″ cake pans. Cream butter and sugar until light and fluffy. Beat in eggs, then fold in flour, baking powder, and coconut. Turn mixture into prepared pans, level surface, and bake at 350°F about 15 minutes, or until just firm to the touch. Cool on a wire rack. Leave until cold.

For the filling Place dates and water in a saucepan and simmer 10-15 minutes, or until soft. Blend together egg yolks, sugar, milk, and cornstarch. Off the heat, stir mixture into dates and return to heat. Simmer, stirring frequently, about 5 minutes. Let cool, then beat in butter. Sandwich the two cakes together with about a third of the mixture, and use remainder to cover top and sides.

For the topping Press toasted coconut over the surface of the gâteau. Cut dates in half lengthwise, remove the pits, then glaze dates with honey. Arrange on top of cake.

Carrot cake

In this Cranks variation of a traditional Swiss recipe the addition of carrots gives the cake a very moist texture.

Medium-sized carrots 2 to 3
Organic eggs 2
Raw sugar ⅔ cup
Oil ½ cup
100% whole wheat flour 1 cup
1½ tsp baking powder
Ground cinnamon 1 tsp
Ground nutmeg ½ tsp
Dried coconut ⅔ cup
Raisins ⅓ cup

Orange icing
Butter or margarine 3 tbsp
Raw sugar ½ cup
Orange, grated rind of ½
Shelled walnuts, chopped 3 tbsp

Grease and flour the base of a 7″ square cake pan. Finely grate carrots. Whisk eggs and sugar together until thick and creamy. Whisk in oil slowly, then add remaining ingredients and mix together to combine evenly. Spoon mixture into prepared pan. Level surface and bake at 375°F 20-25 minutes, or until firm to the touch and golden brown. Cool on a wire rack. Spread with orange icing when cold.

For the icing Beat butter until soft, then beat in sugar and orange rind. Spread over the cake and sprinkle with chopped walnuts.

Honey cake

Honey ¾ cup
Butter or margarine 2 tbsp
100% whole wheat flour 1½ cup
Salt, pinch
Allspice ½ tsp
Ground nutmeg ¼ tsp
Ground cinnamon ¼ tsp
Organic egg 1
Baking soda ¾ tsp
Milk 3 tbsp
Slivered almonds 3 tbsp

Heat honey and butter together until butter has melted. Off the heat, beat in flour, salt, spices, and egg. Blend baking soda and milk together and stir into mixture. Turn into a 9″ greased cake pan. Sprinkle surface with slivered almonds and bake at 350°F 25-30 minutes, or until golden and firm to the touch. Cool slightly before turning out onto a wire rack.

Poppyseed cake

Poppyseeds are usually thought of only as a decoration in baking, but this recipe proves their worth as a main ingredient.

Poppyseeds ⅔ cup
Milk ⅔ cup
Organic eggs 2
Raw sugar ⅔ cup
Oil ½ cup
Almond extract 1 tsp
100% whole wheat flour 2 cups
3 tsp baking powder
Skim milk powder ½ cup
Ground cinnamon 1 tsp

Grease and flour the base of an 11 x 7" cake pan. Soak two-thirds of the poppyseeds in milk 1 hour. Whisk eggs and sugar together until light and creamy. Very slowly whisk in oil and almond extract until thoroughly mixed. Fold in remaining ingredients. Pour mixture into prepared pan, sprinkle with remaining poppyseeds and bake at 375°F 20-25 minutes, or until just firm to the touch. Cool on a wire rack. Cut into slices to serve.

Walnut sandwich cake

Butter or margarine 8 tbsp
Raw sugar ⅔ cup
Organic eggs 2
100% whole wheat flour 1¼ cups
1½ tsp baking powder
Walnuts, chopped ½ cup
Warm water 1 tbsp

Filling
Butter, softened 4 tbsp
Raw sugar ⅓ cup
Walnuts, chopped 2 tbsp

Grease and line the base of two 7" cake pans. Cream butter and sugar together until light and fluffy. Beat in eggs, one at a time, then fold in remaining ingredients. Divide mixture between prepared pans, level surface, and bake at 375°F 15-20 minutes, or until risen and firm to the touch. Cool on a wire rack.

For the filling Cream butter and sugar together until pale and fluffy. Stir in walnuts. Use half the mixture and sandwich the two cakes together. Use remaining filling to decorate the top of the cake.

Simnel cake

A special fruit cake originally made to celebrate Laetare Sunday, and now generally associated with Easter.

Butter or margarine 8 oz
Raw sugar 1⅓ cups
Organic eggs 4
100% whole wheat flour 2½ cups
Salt, pinch
Currants 2 cups
Golden seedless raisins 1 cup
Lemon, grated rind of 1
Ground cinnamon 1 tsp
Ground nutmeg 1 tsp
Milk to mix
Mock marzipan (*see page 139*) 1½ lb
Apricot jam

Grease and flour an 8″ round cake pan. Cream butter and sugar until pale and fluffy. Beat in eggs one at a time. Combine flour, salt, currants, raisins, lemon rind, and spices and fold into creamed mixture. Add sufficient milk to give a "dropping" consistency. Spoon half of the cake mixture into prepared pan. Level surface. Roll out one third of marzipan to an 8″ round. Place on top of cake mixture. Top with remaining cake mixture and level surface. Bake at 300°F about 2½ hours, or until firm to the touch. Cool in the pan.

The next day roll out half of the remaining marzipan to an 8″ round. Brush with apricot jam and press on to top of cake. Flute edges and, with a knife, mark a lattice effect on top. Use remaining paste to make 11 balls. Position these on the edge of the cake by using a little apricot jam.

Orange cake

Butter or margarine 8 tbsp
Raw sugar ⅔ cup
Small orange, grated rind & juice of 1
100% whole wheat flour 1 cup
1½ tsp baking powder
Salt, pinch
Water 1 tbsp
Organic eggs, separated 2

Icing
Butter or margarine 4 tbsp
Raw sugar ½ cup
Small orange, grated rind & juice of 1
Walnuts, chopped, to decorate

Grease and flour the base of two 7″ cake pans. Cream butter and sugar until light and fluffy. Beat in orange rind and juice and egg yolks. Fold in flour, baking powder, and salt. Whisk egg whites until stiff and fold into cake mixture. Divide mixture between prepared pans. Level surface. Bake at 350°F about 15 minutes, or until risen and just firm to the touch. Cool on a wire rack.

For the icing Cream butter and sugar until really pale and fluffy. Beat in orange rind and juice. Use half the icing to sandwich cakes together. Spread remaining icing over the top of the cake. Decorate edge with chopped walnuts.

Date & walnut loaf

The combination of date and walnut gives this cake a particularly good flavor, especially if it's spread with butter.

Butter or margarine 10 tbsp
Raw sugar ¾ cup
Organic eggs, beaten 3
Small orange, grated rind & juice of 1
Pitted dates, chopped 1 cup
Walnuts, chopped ⅔ cup
100% whole wheat flour 2½ cups
3½ tsp baking powder

Cream butter and sugar together until pale and fluffy. Beat in eggs a little at a time. Stir in orange rind. Fold in dates, two-thirds of the walnuts, baking powder and flour, and lastly stir in orange juice. Spoon mixture into a greased and floured 5 x 9 inch loaf pan. Level surface, then sprinkle over the remaining chopped walnuts. Bake at 325°F 1-1¼ hours, or until risen and golden brown.

Orange gingercake

Gingercake is often considered to be one of the most difficult cakes to make, so follow this recipe carefully to ensure good results.

100% whole wheat flour 2 cups
Ground ginger 1½ tsp
Baking powder 1½ tsp
Baking soda ½ tsp
Salt ½ tsp
Raw sugar 1⅓ cups
Molasses 2 tbsp
Butter or margarine 6 tbsp
Milk 4 tbsp
Organic egg 1
Small orange, grated rind of 1
Orange juice 2 tbsp

Grease and flour base of an 11 x 7″ shallow cake pan. Put the first 5 ingredients in a mixing bowl. Heat together sugar, molasses, and butter until butter is melted. Combine all the ingredients together, beat well, and pour into prepared pan. Bake at 325°F about ½ hour, or until just firm to the touch. Cool in pan, then cut into squares.

Fruit cake without eggs (vegan)

This fruit cake, which was created for vegans, does not contain butter, eggs, or milk and therefore has more limited keeping qualities.

Mixed currants & raisins 4½ cups
Water 2 cups
Oil ½ cup
100% whole wheat flour 3 cups
4½ tsp baking powder

Grease and flour a 7½″ round cake pan. Place all the ingredients, except the sherry, in a bowl and beat well until evenly mixed. Pour into prepared pan and bake at 300°F about 2 hours, or until risen and firm to the touch. Allow to cool slightly in the pan, then spoon

Blanched almonds, chopped ½
   cup
Molasses 1 tbsp
Lemon, grated rind of 1
Allspice 2 tsp
Raw sugar ½ cup
Sherry or rum (optional)
   3 tbsp

sherry over cake and leave in pan until completely cold.

Unlike a traditional fruit cake, this cake does not keep for very long.

Barabrith

Based on the traditional Welsh recipe, this is similar to a tea bread and should always be served buttered.

Mixed dried fruit 2 cups
Raw sugar ½ cup
Lemon, grated rind of ½
Hot tea 1¾ cups
100% whole wheat flour 3 cups
Baking powder 2 tsp
Allspice 2 tsp
Organic egg 1

Makes 1 large loaf

Put fruit, sugar, lemon rind, and tea in a bowl. Cover and let soak overnight. Strain fruit and reserve liquid. Put remaining ingredients into a mixing bowl, add fruit and enough liquid to mix to a soft "dropping" consistency–you may need to use all the liquid. Pour into a greased and floured loaf pan. Bake at 375°F 45-50 minutes, or until risen and firm to the touch. Cool on a wire rack. Serve sliced and buttered.

Whole wheat muffins

These light-textured cakes, which are best served warm from the oven, are ideal for breakfast or with morning coffee.

100% whole wheat flour 2 cups
Barley flour 1 cup
Baking powder 1 tsp
Salt ½ tsp
Raw sugar ⅔ cup
Butter or margarine 1 oz
Golden seedless raisins ⅔ cup
Milk 1 cup
Honey or molasses 2 tbsp
Baking soda 1 tsp

Makes 18 muffins

Grease muffin tins for 18 muffins. In a bowl combine flours, baking powder, salt, and sugar. Rub in butter and add raisins. Warm milk and honey together until honey is dissolved. Stir in baking soda and stir liquid into dry ingredients, beating well. Spoon mixture into pans and bake at 400°F 15-20 minutes, or until risen and firm to the touch. Serve warm with butter.

Bran muffins

100% whole wheat flour 3½
  cups
Bran ½ cup
Baking powder 1 tsp
Salt ½ tsp
Raw sugar ⅔ cup
Butter or margarine 1 oz
Milk 1 cup
Honey or molasses 2 tbsp
Baking soda 1 tsp

Makes 18 muffins

Grease muffin tins for 18 muffins. In a bowl combine flour, bran, baking powder, salt, and sugar. Rub in butter or margarine. Heat milk and honey together, then add to dry ingredients with baking soda. Beat well. Spoon mixture into prepared pans and bake at 400°F 15-20 minutes, or until risen and firm to the touch. Serve warm.

Apple cakes

Rich, unusual, and quickly made cakes.

Medium-sized cooking apples 2
100% whole wheat flour 2 cups
Salt, pinch
Ground cinnamon ½ tsp
Baking powder 1 tsp
Butter or margarine 6 oz
Raw sugar ⅓ cup
Organic egg, beaten 1

Makes 12 buns

Core and dice apples. Combine flour, salt, spice, and baking powder in a bowl. Rub in butter until mixture resembles fine crumbs, then add remaining ingredients and combine well together. Place heaped spoonfuls on a lightly greased baking sheet and bake at 375°F 20-25 minutes, or until golden. Cool slightly before transferring to a wire rack.

Old English rock buns

The term "rock" suggests the appearance and not the texture of these small cakes!

100% whole wheat flour 2 cups
Salt, pinch
3 tsp baking powder
Allspice 1 tsp
Butter or margarine 4 oz
Raw sugar ½ cup
Currants ⅓ cup
Organic egg 1
Milk 2 tbsp
Lemon, grated rind of ½

Makes about 8 buns

Combine flour, salt, baking powder, and spice in a bowl. Rub butter into flour, and then mix in sugar and fruit. Beat egg and add to mixture; stir well. Add milk and stir to give a soft but firm dough. Form into "rocky" shapes and place on a greased baking sheet. Bake at 375°F about 15 minutes, or until just brown. Cool slightly on the baking sheet before transferring to a wire rack. Store in an airtight container.

Raspberry buns

100% whole wheat flour 3 cups
4½ tsp baking powder
Ground nutmeg ½ tsp
Butter or margarine 4 oz
Raw sugar ⅔ cup
Currants ⅓ cup
Organic egg 1
Milk 2-3 tbsp
Raspberry jam 4 tbsp

Makes 12 buns

Put flour, baking powder, and nutmeg in a bowl, and rub in butter until mixture resembles fine crumbs. Stir in sugar and currants. Beat egg and add to dry ingredients with enough milk to form a firm dough. Roll dough into 12 balls. Place on a lightly greased baking sheet. Press a well in the center of each bun and fill with jam. Bake at 375°F about 20 minutes, or until firm and golden. Cool on a wire rack.

Walnut bars

Soft and chewy textured pieces of cake with coarsely chopped walnuts added—quite delicious!

Oil 3 tbsp
Molasses 1 tbsp
Raw sugar ⅔ cup
Shelled walnuts, chopped ¾ cup
Organic eggs 2
Vanilla extract 2 tsp
Wheat germ 1 cup
Salt ¼ tsp
Skim milk powder ⅔ cup
Baking powder ½ tsp

Makes about 16 bars

Beat together the first 8 ingredients, then sift in milk powder and baking powder. Beat well, then pour into a greased and floured 8" square shallow cake pan. Bake at 350°F 25-30 minutes, or until just firm to the touch. Cut into bars while still warm.

"Chocolate" éclairs

Choux pastry (see page 181)
  1 recipe
Heavy cream ½ cup

Carob icing
Carob bar 2.8 oz
Butter or margarine 1 oz

Makes about 12 éclairs

Lightly grease 2 baking sheets. Using a pastry bag fitted with a ½" plain nozzle, pipe choux pastry into 2½" lengths. (If you do not have a pastry bag, it is possible to spoon the choux pastry on to the baking sheets and although this does not give as professional a finish, the result is perfectly acceptable.) Bake at 425°F 20-25 minutes, or until risen and golden brown. They should be hollow and fairly dry. Make a slit in the side of each éclair with the tip of a knife. Cool on a wire rack.

For the icing Melt carob bar and butter together over low heat. Whip cream until it holds its shape and use to fill éclairs, then dip in carob icing, drawing each one across the surface of the icing and lifting to release it. Leave to set.

Fruit scones

Fruit scones are baked every morning in Cranks bakeries and are extremely popular with our customers at coffee time and with teas in Cranks Dartington restaurant.

100% whole wheat flour 2 cups
Salt, pinch
3 tsp baking powder
Butter or margarine 6 tbsp
Raw sugar 2 tbsp
Golden seedless raisins ½ cup
Milk, about ½ cup

Makes 8 scones

Put flour, baking powder, and salt in a bowl. Rub in butter until mixture resembles fine crumbs. Stir in sugar and raisins, then add enough milk for a soft, manageable dough. Knead gently on a lightly floured surface, then roll out about ¾" thick. Stamp out 3" rounds and roll to make remaining scones. Place fairly close together on a lightly greased baking sheet and bake at 425°F 10-15 minutes, or until golden. Cool on a wire rack. Best eaten on the day of making.

Drop scones

Sometimes known as Scottish griddle scones, these are made from a rich batter that is dropped in spoonfuls on to a hot greased griddle to cook. Serve straight from the griddle with butter or honey.

100% whole wheat flour 1 cup
Raw sugar 2 tbsp
1½ tsp baking powder
Organic egg 1
Milk, about ½ cup

Makes about 12 scones

Beat all ingredients together in a mixing bowl to give a fairly thick pouring consistency. Heat a griddle or frying pan to medium heat, brush lightly with oil or melted butter, and drop spoonfuls of the mixture on to griddle. Leave until bubbles appear on the surface and a "skin" starts to form. Turn with a spatula and cook until golden brown on the second side.

Cheese scones

Traditionally Cranks cheese scones are clover-shaped, and that's how you will see them in all the Cranks shops. At home a fluted round cutter would do well.

100% whole wheat flour 4 cups
Baking powder 2 tbsp
Salt, large pinch
Cayenne, large pinch
Butter or margarine 4 tbsp
Cheddar cheese, grated 2½ cups
Milk, about 1 cup

Makes 15 scones

Put flour, baking powder, salt, and cayenne in a bowl. Rub in butter until mixture resembles fine crumbs. Stir in 2 cups cheese and enough milk to give a soft, manageable dough. Knead gently, then roll out to 1" thickness. Stamp out 3" rounds with a fluted cutter. Brush with milk and sprinkle with a little of the remaining cheese. Bake at 400°F about 20 minutes, or until golden. Cool on a wire rack.

Raw sugar meringues

Meringues are popular with all ages, and using raw sugar gives them a particularly good taste. Sandwiched together with cream they are ideal for tea or as a dessert. It is advisable to sift the sugar before using it to remove any lumps.

Egg whites 6
Salt, pinch
Raw sugar 2 cups
Heavy cream 1 cup

Makes about 20 meringues

Stiffly whisk egg whites with salt until they stand in peaks. Gradually whisk in sugar a spoonful at a time until mixture is stiff again. Drop spoonfuls of mixture on to baking sheets lined with parchment paper.

If wished, you can pipe shapes with a pastry bag fitted with a star nozzle. Bake at 250°F 3-4 hours, or until completely dried out and crisp. Just before serving, whip cream and use to sandwich meringues together.

Welsh butter cakes

These are an extremely rich form of griddle scone. Handle with care when cooking as the dough is delicate.

100% whole wheat flour 2¼ cups
Baking powder ½ tsp
Ground nutmeg ½ tsp
Butter or margarine 12 tbsp
Raw sugar ½ cup
Currants ½ cup
Organic egg 1

Makes about 10 cakes

Put flour in a mixing bowl with baking powder and nutmeg. Rub in butter, then add remaining ingredients and work mixture together for a soft manageable dough. Roll out about ½" thick on a lightly floured board. Stamp out 3" rounds. Lightly butter a griddle or frying pan and cook cakes on both sides over medium heat about 5 minutes until golden. Serve warm.

Coconut castles

Egg whites 2
Raw sugar ⅔ cup
Dried coconut 1 cup
Almond extract ½ tsp

Makes 8 castles

Whisk egg whites and sugar together until just frothy. Stir in coconut and almond extract and shape mixture into 8 "castles." Place on a greased baking sheet and bake at 325°F about 35 minutes, or until golden. Cool on a wire rack.

Honey buns

An unusual recipe with an interesting result. These honey buns are deliciously sticky. Try serving them warm with vanilla ice cream.

Oil ¾ cup
Raw sugar ½ cup
Fresh orange juice ½ cup
100% whole wheat flour 4 cups
Baking powder 2 tsp
Lemon, grated rind of ½
Shelled walnuts, coarsely
   chopped ½ cup

Place oil, sugar, orange juice, flour, baking powder, and lemon rind in a bowl. Work together to give a soft dough. Shape into 12 ovals and press each one into chopped walnuts. Place walnut-side up on a greased baking sheet. Bake at 375°F about 20 minutes, or until golden and just firm to the touch. Meanwhile, put ingredients for syrup into a saucepan. Place over

Syrup
Honey ½ cup
Water ½ cup
Raw sugar ½ cup

Makes 12 buns

gentle heat, stirring occasionally, until sugar is dissolved. Bring to a boil and boil 5 minutes. Spoon mixture over buns on baking sheet and let soak 15 minutes, or until syrup is absorbed. Cool on a wire rack covered with waxed paper.

Truffle triangle

This lovely no-cook cake has a flavor that can be varied with the type of cake used to make the crumb base.

Leftover cake 1½ lb
Raw sugar mincemeat or apricot jam ½ cup
Shelled walnuts, chopped ½ cup
Carob powder ½ cup
*Orange juice, sherry, or rum 3-4 tbsp
Slivered almonds, toasted 4 tbsp to decorate

*The quantity of liquid will vary with the type of cake crumbs used–add enough to give a moist yet firm consistency.

Carob Icing
Heavy cream 5 tbsp
Carob bar 2.8 oz

Crumble cake into a bowl, add mincemeat, walnuts, and carob powder and enough liquid to give a moist, yet firm consistency. Work mixture together until fairly smooth. Turn mixture on to a working surface and press into a triangular log shape. Place cake on a wire rack with a baking sheet underneath.

For the icing Bring cream to a boil, reduce heat. Break carob bar into pieces and add to cream. Stir over gentle heat until completely melted and smooth.

Carefully spoon icing over truffle triangle. Collect icing that has run on to tray, warm it gently, and repeat coating process. Sprinkle slivered almonds on top and let set. Serve cut in slices.

BISCUITS

There are few products that so clearly illuminate the difference between whole wheat and bleached white flour as biscuits. Who could possibly opt for the flaccid white offering when presented with the option of the whole wheat biscuit with its warmth of color, textural character, and, of course, the incomparable nutty flavor of the "real" food product?

One has to be honest and admit that a biscuit is really an unnecessary food, perhaps the ultimate snack, but we should not be too purist and we can admit the pleasure of the addition of a crisp tasty biscuit to the equally unnecessary but pleasurable social pause for a cup of coffee or tea.

In Cranks we store the biscuits appropriately in metal biscuit tins where they keep fresh for several days, but a sealed plastic bag is almost as good, provided the biscuits have been thoroughly cooled first.

Cranks flapjack

Butter or margarine 10 tbsp
Raw sugar ½ cup
Molasses 3 tbsp
Oatmeal 2 cups
Salt, pinch

Makes 12 pieces

Melt butter, sugar, and molasses in a pan–do not let it boil. Mix in oatmeal and salt and stir thoroughly. Press into an 8″ square pan and smooth over surface with a spatula. Bake at 375°F 25-30 minutes, or until set and golden brown. Mark into portions while still warm, then let cool on a wire rack. Store in an airtight container.

Melting moments

So called because they melt in the mouth.

Butter or margarine 10 tbsp
Raw sugar ½ cup
Beaten egg 1 tbsp
Vanilla extract ½ tsp
100% whole wheat flour 1 cup
1½ tsp baking powder
Oats, *rolled* ¼ cup
Extra oats to coat

Makes 12-14 biscuits

Cream butter and sugar until light and fluffy. Beat in egg and vanilla extract. Work in flour, baking powder, and rolled oats. Form mixture into balls the size of a walnut, and coat with rolled oats. Place well apart on a greased baking sheet and flatten slightly. Bake at 350°F 15-20 minutes, or until golden. Cool slightly before transferring to a wire rack.

Eccles cakes

Whole wheat shortcrust pastry
 (*see page 181*) 14 oz
Currants ⅔ cup
Lemon, coarsely grated rind of 1
Orange, coarsely grated rind of
 1
Allspice ½ tsp
Nutmeg ½ tsp
Raw sugar ⅓ cup
Butter or margarine 1 oz
Egg white 1
Raw sugar to decorate

Makes 10 cakes

Roll out pastry and use to stamp out ten 4″ rounds. Mix together currants, orange and lemon rind, and spices. Melt sugar and butter together and stir in fruit. Cool. Put a spoonful of mixture in the center of each piece of pastry. Bring edges together over filling and seal firmly by pinching together. Turn over and press lightly to flatten. Place on a lightly greased baking sheet. Make a lattice pattern with a knife on top of each cake. Brush with beaten egg white and sprinkle with sugar. Bake at 425°F 15 minutes. Cool on a wire rack.

Date slices

Cooked pitted dates sandwiched between an oaty mixture and baked until golden.

Dates (or dried apricots or figs)
    chopped 2 cups
Water 6 tbsp
Lemon, grated rind of ½
100% whole wheat flour 2 cups
Oatmeal 1 cup
Raw sugar ½ cup
Butter or margarine, melted
    10 tbsp

Makes 16 slices

Put dates, water, and lemon rind in a saucepan. Heat gently, stirring occasionally, until mixture is soft. Combine remaining ingredients and sprinkle half the mixture into an 11 x 7" shallow cake pan and press down well. Cover with dates and sprinkle remaining oat mixture over and press down firmly. Bake at 400°F 20 minutes. Cool in pan and then cut into slices.

Carob crunch

A rich, crunchy biscuit that has been made in Cranks for over twenty years.

Butter or margarine, melted
    8 tbsp
Carob powder 2 tsp
100% whole wheat flour 1 cup
Baking powder 1 tsp
Raw sugar ⅓ cup
Dried coconut ⅔ cup

Makes 8 biscuits

Melt butter in a saucepan and stir in carob powder. Add remaining ingredients and mix together. Press mixture into a 7" square cake pan and smooth over with a spatula. Bake at 375°F 25 minutes, or until just set and golden. Mark into wedges while still hot, and allow to cool before taking out of pan.

For special occasions coat with CAROB ICING (*see page 152*).

Shortbread

Butter or margarine 8 tbsp
100% whole wheat flour 1½
    cups
Raw sugar ⅓ cup

Makes 8 pieces

Cut butter into flour with a pastry blender and rub in until mixture resembles breadcrumbs, then add sugar. Work mixture together to give a firm dough. Press into a 7" round pan, neaten edges with a fork, and use prongs to make a decorative pattern. Mark into 8 portions and bake at 300°F about 45 minutes. Cut into pieces while warm, but let cool in pan.

The same mixture can be used for making individual biscuits.

For special occasions coat with CAROB ICING (*see page 152*).

Country biscuits

Classic biscuits with a wholesome nutty texture, so versatile that they can be served with sweet or savoury foods.

100% whole wheat flour 1½ cups
Coarse oatmeal ⅓ cup
Baking powder 1 tsp
Salt ½ tsp
Butter or margarine 6 tbsp
Raw sugar ⅓ cup
Milk (or soy milk) to mix 3 tbsp

Makes about 18 biscuits

Mix all dry ingredients, except sugar, together. Rub in butter until mixture resembles fine crumbs, stir in sugar, and add milk. Stir well until dough is firm but manageable. Roll out fairly thinly on a lightly floured board and stamp out 3" rounds. Place on a greased baking sheet and bake at 350°F 20-25 minutes, until light brown. Cool on a wire rack and store in an airtight container.

Try sandwiching the biscuits together with jam in the middle—ideal for children.

Coconut biscuits

Butter or margarine 8 tbsp
100% whole wheat flour 1 cup
1½ tsp baking powder
Raw sugar ⅔ cup
Dried coconut ⅔ cup
Salt, pinch
Organic egg 1

Makes about 20 biscuits

Rub butter into flour and baking powder until mixture resembles fine crumbs, then stir in sugar, coconut, and salt. Mix well, stir in egg, then mix to a soft dough. Roll out fairly thinly on a lightly floured board and stamp into 3" rounds. Place on greased baking sheet. Bake at 350°F about 15 minutes, or until golden brown. Cool on a wire rack and store in an airtight container.

Carob chip cookies

A whole food version of chocolate chip cookies.

Butter or margarine 12 tbsp
100% whole wheat flour 2 cups
3 tsp baking powder
Raw sugar ⅔ cup
Salt, pinch
Organic egg 1
Carob bar, chopped 2.8 oz

Makes 15 cookies

Rub butter into flour and baking powder until mixture resembles fine crumbs. Add sugar, salt, and egg and mix well. Stir in carob chips and mix to a soft dough. Chill dough for ½ hour, then roll out on a lightly floured surface to ¼" thickness. Stamp out 3½" rounds and place well apart on lightly greased baking sheets. Mark with prongs of a fork. Bake at 350°F 10-12 minutes, or until golden. Cool slightly, then transfer to a wire rack.

Florentines

These are easy to prepare, but care must be taken when cooling, removing from the parchment paper, and storing as these biscuits are delicate.

Butter or margarine 6 tbsp
Raw sugar ⅔ cup
Shelled walnuts, chopped ¾ cup
Slivered almonds ½ cup
Dried fruit, e.g., pitted dates,
   raisins, chopped ⅓ cup
100% whole wheat flour 1 tbsp

Makes 12 biscuits

Melt butter and sugar together in a saucepan over low heat. Add remaining ingredients. Line baking sheets with parchment paper and drop large spoonfuls of the mixture well apart on prepared sheets. Press into neat shapes. Bake at 350°F 12-15 minutes, or until golden. Leave until cold before removing from paper.

Sesame thins

Baked sesame seeds give these crisp, golden biscuits a unique flavor.

100% whole wheat flour 1 cup
Butter or margarine 8 tbsp
Sesame seeds ½ cup
Raw sugar ⅓ cup

Makes 12 biscuits

Put flour in a bowl and rub in butter. Add sesame seeds and sugar and work mixture together. Press mixture into an 11 x 7" shallow cake pan. Bake at 350°F about 20 minutes, or until golden. Mark into slices while warm but leave to cool in pan.

Millet & peanut cookies

A recipe specially devised for this book, but since their introduction into Cranks shops these cookies have become a great favorite.

Oil 4 tbsp
Salt ¼ tsp
Organic egg 1
Raw sugar ½ cup
Peanuts, ground ¾ cup
Raisins ½ cup
Millet flakes ½ cup

Makes 10 cookies

Lightly whisk together oil, salt, egg, and sugar. Stir in remaining ingredients until well blended. Roll mixture into 10 balls. Place on a lightly greased baking sheet. Press each one down to flatten slightly. Bake at 350°F about 15 minutes, or until golden. Allow to cool on baking sheet for a few minutes before transferring to a wire rack.

Caraway bran biscuits

An old-fashioned recipe with a distinctive flavor.

Butter or margarine 4 tbsp
Raw sugar ⅓ cup
100% whole wheat flour 1 cup
1½ tsp baking powder
Bran ½ cup
Caraway seeds 1 tbsp
Organic egg 1

Makes about 18 biscuits

Cream butter and sugar together until light and fluffy. Add flour, baking powder, bran, caraway seeds, and egg and work together to form a soft dough. Roll out fairly thinly on a lightly floured surface and stamp out 3″ rounds. Place on a greased baking sheet and bake at 350°F 10-15 minutes, or until golden. Cool on a wire rack and store in an airtight container.

Crunchies

Butter or margarine 8 tbsp
Raw sugar ⅔ cup
100% whole wheat flour 1½ cups
1¾ tsp baking powder
Crunchy breakfast cereal ½ cup
Currants 2 tbsp
Molasses 1 tbsp
Allspice ½ tsp

Makes 10 biscuits

Melt butter in a saucepan. Off the heat, stir in all remaining ingredients until evenly blended. Press mixture into 10 even-sized balls and place well apart on a lightly greased baking sheet. Bake at 350°F 12-15 minutes. Allow to cool slightly on baking sheet before transferring to a wire rack.

Peanut rounds

Butter or margarine 8 tbsp
Raw sugar 1 cup
Organic egg 1
Peanut butter ¾ cup
Peanuts, coarsely chopped ⅔ cup
100% whole wheat flour ¾ cup
Baking powder ½ tsp
Flaked wheat 3¼ cups

Makes about 25 biscuits

Cream butter and sugar together until light and fluffy. Beat in egg, then add remaining ingredients and work mixture together to give a manageable dough. Roll out fairly thinly on a lightly floured surface and stamp out 3″ rounds with a fluted cutter. Place on a greased baking sheet and bake at 375°F about 15 minutes, or until golden. Cool on a wire rack. Store in an airtight container.

Gingernuts

Really dark crunchy biscuits.

Butter or margarine 5 tbsp
100% whole wheat flour 1½ cups
1¾ tsp baking powder
Raw sugar ⅓ cup
Molasses 4 tbsp
Baking soda ¾ tsp
Ground ginger 2 tsp

Makes about 15 biscuits

Rub butter into flour and baking powder until mixture resembles fine crumbs. Stir in sugar. Warm molasses in a saucepan, and stir in baking soda and ginger. Add ginger mixture to dry ingredients, and knead well to form a soft dough. Roll mixture into balls about the size of a walnut. Place well apart on oiled baking sheets, flatten slightly. Bake at 350°F about 15 minutes. Allow to cool slightly on baking sheets before transferring to a wire rack.

Cheesejacks

This is a savoury variation of Cranks flapjacks and is particularly popular with children.

Oatmeal 1¼ cups
Cheddar cheese, grated 1½ cups
Organic egg, beaten 1
Butter or margarine, melted
  4 tbsp
Rosemary, crushed ½ tsp
Salt & pepper to taste

Makes 12 slices

Combine all ingredients together. Mix well. Then press into a shallow 7″ square cake pan. Bake at 350°F about 40 minutes, or until golden. Cut into slices. Serve hot or cold.

Cheese biscuits

Mouthwatering savoury biscuits, ideal to serve with drinks.

100% whole wheat flour 1 cup
Butter, softened 8 tbsp
Cheddar cheese, grated 1 cup
Paprika, pinch

Work ingredients together to give a soft, manageable dough. Roll out on a lightly floured surface to ⅛″ thick and stamp out rounds or cut into straws. Bake at 400°F 5-8 minutes, depending on size. Cool on a wire rack.

Day-old whole wheat bread
Vegex

Whole wheat rusks

These thin fingers of bread, flavored with Vegex and baked until crisp, are particularly good for teething babies and young children.

Cut the bread into ½″ fingers. Dilute 1 teaspoon Vegex stirred into 1 cup boiling water. Brush sides and edges of bread with Vegex and bake at 300°F about 1 hour, until really crisp and dried.

Melba toast

Day-old whole wheat bread

Cut bread into wafer-thin slices with a sharp serrated knife. Arrange in a single layer on a baking sheet and bake at 400°F 7-8 minutes, or until really crisp and golden. Cool on a wire rack, then keep in an airtight container.

BREAKFAST CEREALS

It was as long ago as 1926 that Dr. Bircher-Benner published a small book promoting the importance to health of the inclusion of a good proportion of raw food in the diet. One of the uncooked dishes he invented was "Raw fruit porridge" or "Muesli." This became a standard stocked line in health food shops throughout Europe and has recently appeared on the shelves of supermarkets in response to a growing public demand, although one suspects that the product now bears little relation to Dr. Bircher-Benner's original intention. In any case, he stressed the importance of preparing the dish just before it is to be eaten. He believed that the nutritional value of the dish came from the interaction of all the materials united by nature within a single food. In terms of energy, he thought "that this value resided in the calculated and graded play of rainbow colors inside the food, considered as a total combination of the energies of sunlight."

There are, of course, breakfast cereals other than muesli, and it is not necessary to turn to packages of brand-named products when these can so easily be made at home, and with all the "right" ingredients. These home-made cereals can be put together in their dry condition, lightly toasted, and stored in airtight containers for a number of weeks.

Breakfast cereal

Popular with all the family, this delicious crunchy breakfast cereal is a "full of goodness" way to start the day.

Oatmeal 3½ cups
Sunflower seeds ½ cup
Mixed nuts, chopped ¾ cup
Wheat germ ¾ cup
Dried coconut 1 cup
Sesame seeds ¼ cup
Raw sugar ⅔ cup
Water ½ cup
Oil ½ cup
Vanilla extract ½ tsp
Salt ½ tsp

Makes 2¼ lb

Combine the first 7 ingredients in a large mixing bowl. Whisk together water, oil, vanilla, and salt, then stir in dry ingredients. Mix well. Spread cereal over the base of a large, shallow roasting pan and bake at 375°F 20-30 minutes, turning occasionally until crisp and golden. Let cool. Store in an airtight container.

Muesli

The Cranks version of the original Swiss recipe, so versatile that it can be served at any time—not just for breakfast.

Oatmeal 1 cup
Golden seedless raisins 2 tbsp
Fresh orange juice 1 cup
Eating apples, grated 2
Milk to mix
Chopped nuts
Honey

Serves 4-6

Put oatmeal, sultanas, and orange juice in a mixing bowl. Cover and let soak overnight. Stir in apple and enough milk to give a soft consistency. Spoon muesli into dishes and top with chopped nuts and honey.

Milled whole wheat berries & nuts

Wheat berries ⅔ cup
Finely chopped nuts 4 tbsp
Honey to taste
Milk to taste

Serves 6

Pass wheat through a grain mill or grind in a coffee grinder. Mix with nuts and serve with milk and honey as a breakfast cereal.

BREAD

Bread seen as "the staff of life" obviously played a much larger part in mankind's diet in the past than it does today. We would no doubt benefit greatly were we to return to a much simpler mode of living and eating, with bread in its proper central role as provider of health through its abundance of the essential elements. Proteins, carbohydrates, vitamins, minerals, and trace elements are all contained in a living relationship in the 100% whole grain loaf. This is made from flour that has had nothing taken away and nothing added but is just as nature intended!

All Cranks bread, and in fact all Cranks bakery products, are made with only 100% whole grain form of English, compost-grown, stone ground flour. Our bread style, which is close and moist, was originally based on Doris Grant's recipe for a home-produced whole grain loaf. Many of our recipes for other breads simply use the basic whole grain dough and then modify it with the addition of other ingredients such as bran, cheese, eggs, molasses, etc.

Cranks whole wheat bread

This is the Cranks adaptation of Doris Grant's original recipe, which had been invented to help the busy housewife who wanted to make her own bread. It is somewhat unconventional in method as it eliminates kneading.

100% whole wheat flour 12 cups
Sea salt 1 tbsp
Dried yeast 1 tbsp
Raw sugar 1 tbsp
Water 4-5 cups

Makes 3 loaves

For 1 loaf or 6 buns
100% whole wheat flour 4 cups
Sea salt 1 tsp
Dried yeast 1½ tsp
Raw sugar 1 tsp
Water 1-1¾ cups

Mix flour with salt (in very cold weather warm flour slightly, enough to take the chill off). Mix yeast and sugar in a small bowl with ½ cup of the warm water. Leave in a warm place 10 minutes or so to froth up. Pour yeasty liquid into flour and gradually add rest of water. Mix well–by hand is best. Divide dough into three 5 x 9 inch loaf pans (rounds cake pans may be used if necessary), which have first been greased and warmed. Put pans in a warm place, cover with a cloth or oiled plastic wrap, and leave for about 20 minutes to rise, or until the dough is within ½" of the top of the pans. Bake at 400°F about 35-40 minutes. Allow to cool for a few minutes and turn out on to a wire rack.

For buns Roll out dough thickly on a lightly floured surface and stamp out six 4" rounds. Place on a baking sheet, brush lightly with milk, and bake at 400°F 20-25 minutes. Cool on a wire rack. Split and butter–delicious filled with cottage cheese and lettuce.

100% whole wheat flour 2 cups
Cornmeal ¾ cup
Salt ½ tsp
Butter, margarine, or vegetable
    shortening 2 tbsp
Dried yeast 1½ tsp
Raw sugar 1 tsp
Water, about ½ cup
Molasses 1 tbsp

Makes 1 small loaf

Corn & molasses bread

Put flour, cornmeal, and salt in a bowl. Rub in butter. Put yeast and sugar in a small bowl, stir in half the warm water, and leave in a warm place for about 10 minutes, or until frothy. Pour yeast on to flour, add molasses and sufficient water to mix to a soft, but not sticky, dough. Knead gently on a lightly floured surface 5 minutes, then place in a greased 4½ x 8½ inch loaf pan. Make 3 deep cuts lengthwise across top. Cover with oiled plastic wrap and leave in a warm place until bread reaches the top of pan. Bake at 400°F 25-30 minutes. Remove from pan and cool on a wire rack.

Rye bread

Rye bread is not particularly easy to make and practice may be necessary to achieve a good result. However, it is worthwhile to persevere as this bread is crusty on the outside yet soft-textured with a distinctive flavor.

100% whole wheat flour 4 cups
Coarse rye meal (or flour) 1½ cups
Salt 1½ tsp
Caraway seeds 1½ tsp
Butter or margarine 4 tbsp
Dried yeast 1 tbsp
Raw sugar 1 tbsp
Water 1-1¾ cups

Glaze
Water 1 tsp
Raw sugar ½ tsp

Makes 1 large loaf

Combine flour, rye meal, salt, and 1 tsp caraway seeds in a large mixing bowl. Rub butter in until well blended. Mix together yeast, sugar, and ½ cup warm water. Set aside in a warm place until frothy–about minutes. Add frothy liquid to flour with ½ cup water. Work to a soft dough by hand, adding extra water as necessary. Cover and leave 5 minutes. Knead on a lightly floured surface and form dough into a neat corncob shape. Place on a lightly greased baking sheet. Combine water and sugar for the glaze and brush over top of loaf. Sprinkle remaining ½ tsp caraway seeds over. Make 3 long slashes in the top of loaf. Cover with oiled plastic wrap and leave in a warm place until doubled in size. Remove plastic wrap and bake at 400°F 40-50 minutes.

If loaf sounds hollow when tapped on the base, it means it is cooked.

For a softer crust, place a pan of water in the bottom of the oven during cooking.

Bran bread

A basic whole wheat bread dough with added roughage in the form of bran.

100% whole wheat flour 4 cups
Bran ¾ cup
Salt 1 tsp
Butter, margarine, or vegetable shortening 2 tbsp
Dried yeast 1½ tsp
Raw sugar 1 tbsp
Water, about 1 cup

Makes 1 loaf

Combine flour, bran, and salt in a large bowl. Rub in butter until well blended. Mix together yeast, sugar, and half the warm water and leave in a warm place until frothy. Add yeast mixture to flour and mix together, adding sufficient warm water to give a soft, but not sticky, dough. Cover and let rest 5 minutes. Knead on a lightly floured surface, then press into a greased 5 x 9 inch loaf pan. Cut 2 slashes in the top. Cover with oiled plastic wrap and leave in a warm

place to rise until mixture reaches top of pan. Bake at 400°F 40-50 minutes. Cool on a wire rack.

Barley bread

Barley flour produces a light textured bread, pale in color and unusual in flavor.

Follow the method for BRAN BREAD (see previous recipe).

Barley flour 2 cups
Salt 1 tsp
Dried yeast 1½ tsp
Raw sugar 1 tsp
Water, up to 1 cup

Makes 1 loaf

Soy bread

100% whole wheat flour 3½ cups
Soy flour ½ cup
Salt 1 tsp
Raw sugar 1 tsp
Dried yeast 1½ tsp
Water, about ¾ cup

Makes 1 loaf

Put flours and salt in a mixing bowl. Take 2 large spoonfuls of flour and mix with sugar, yeast, and half the warm water. Leave in a warm place about 20 minutes, or until frothy. Combine all ingredients together and mix to a soft dough. On a lightly floured surface, knead dough for a few minutes, then shape and place in a greased 4½ x 8½ inch loaf pan. Brush top of dough with oil, cover with oiled plastic wrap and put in a warm place until dough comes to top of pan. Bake at 400°F 25-30 minutes. Cool on a wire rack.

Sourdough bread

This unusual method of breadmaking produces a sharp-flavored loaf.

Dried yeast 1 tbsp
Water 4 cups
Raw sugar 1 tsp
100% whole wheat flour 16 cups
Salt 1 tbsp
Oil 3 tbsp

Makes 3 loaves

Mix yeast, 1 cup warm water, sugar, and 2 cups flour to a smooth paste. Cover and leave to "sour" at room temperature for up to 5 days. Put 12 cups flour and remaining water into a large bowl, stir in the soured starter and mix well to a soft dough. Cover with a wet dish towel and leave in a warm place 8 hours or overnight. Beat well, then stir in remaining

ingredients. Knead 5 minutes on a lightly floured surface. Divide mixture between three 5 x 9 inch oiled loaf pans. Cover with oiled plastic wrap and leave in a warm place to rise until doubled in size. Bake at 400°F 35-40 minutes. Cool on a wire rack.

Instead of making a fresh starter each time, it is possible to reserve some of the dough in the refrigerator and to use this as the starter for more loaves as needed.

Cheese bread

Organic egg, beaten 1
Cheddar cheese, grated 2 cups
Whole wheat bread dough, using 4 cups flour (see page 169)

Makes 1 large loaf

Work egg and cheese into dough. Place dough in a lightly greased 5 x 9 inch loaf pan. Continue as for CRANKS WHOLE WHEAT BREAD (see page 169).

Garlic bread

This is delicious served hot with soups and salads.

Garlic cloves, crushed 3
Whole wheat bread dough, using 4 cups flour (see page 169)

Makes 1 large loaf

Knead garlic into dough. Continue as for CRANKS WHOLE WHEAT BREAD (see page 169).

Cheese buns

This is one of the most popular of all Cranks recipes. The buns can be served split, buttered, and filled with beansprouts.

Organic egg, beaten 1
Whole wheat bread dough, using 4 cups flour (see page 169)
Cheddar cheese, grated 2¼ cups

Makes 6 buns

Work egg into dough until evenly mixed. Roll out dough on a lightly floured surface to a rectangle 15 x 10″. Sprinkle a third of cheese over center third of dough. Fold left-hand third of dough over cheese.

Sprinkle another third of cheese over double thickness of dough, then fold right-hand side of dough towards center to cover cheese completely. Press down well. Stamp out 4" rounds, folding and rolling trimmings to make the last buns. Place on floured baking sheet and brush lightly with milk. Sprinkle with remaining cheese and bake at 400°F about 25 minutes. Cool on a wire rack.

Herb bread

An interesting variation of whole wheat bread that adds extra flavor to sandwiches.

Whole wheat bread dough, using 4 cups flour *(see page 169)*
Oregano 1 tsp
Rosemary 1½ tsp
Turmeric (optional) 1 tsp
Sage ½ tsp

Makes 1 loaf

Knead all ingredients together until evenly distributed. Continue as for CRANKS WHOLE WHEAT BREAD *(see page 169)*.

Granary loaf

Granary bread has become so popular in the last few years because of its nutty flavor and texture.

100% whole wheat flour 4 cups
Rye flour ½ cup
Cracked wheat ⅔ cup
Salt 1 tsp

Combine flours, cracked wheat, and salt. Continue as for CRANKS WHOLE WHEAT BREAD *(see page 169)*, adding molasses with water. On a floured surface knead lightly and shape into 2 rounds. Place on greased

Dried yeast 1½ tsp
Raw sugar 1 tsp
Molasses 1 tbsp
Water, about 2 cups
Cracked wheat, to sprinkle

Makes 2 loaves

baking sheets. Brush with water or milk and sprinkle with cracked wheat. Let rise in a warm place until doubled in size–about 45 minutes. Bake at 400°F about 30 minutes.

Four-grain bread

Rye flour 1 cup
Barley flour ½ cup
100% whole wheat flour 1 cup
Oatmeal 1 cup
Salt 1 tsp
Dried yeast 1½ tsp
Raw sugar 1 tsp
Water, about ¾ cup

Makes 1 loaf

Put the first 5 ingredients into a bowl. Take a few spoonfuls of flour mixture and mix with yeast, sugar, and half the warm water. Leave in a warm place until frothy–about 20 minutes. Combine all ingredients together, adding enough warm water to give a soft, manageable dough. Knead well on a lightly floured surface, then put into a 5 x 9 inch oiled loaf pan. Cover and let rise until mixture reaches the top of the pan. Bake at 400°F 35-40 minutes. Cool on a wire rack.

Pumpernickel

An unusual bread that is steamed in a pudding mold rather than baked. Steaming and the absence of yeast produce a close-textured loaf.

*Rye flour 8 cups
Salt 2 tbsp
Hot water 2½-3½ cups
Molasses 4 tbsp

Makes 2 loaves

Put flour and salt in a bowl. Mix molasses with 2 cups water and add to flour. Mix well, adding extra water if necessary to give a soft dough. Divide mixture between 2 well-greased molds (molds should be three-quarters full).

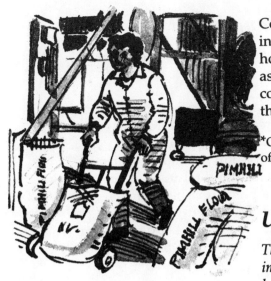

Cover with buttered waxed paper or foil, with a pleat in it to allow for expansion. Place molds in a pan of hot water. Cover and simmer up to 5 hours. Refill pan as necessary. Turn out and cool on a wire rack. When cold, wrap in waxed paper and refrigerate. Serve thinly sliced.

*Other coarse flours may be used to vary the color and flavor of the finished loaves.

Unyeasted bread

This dough will not rise like a traditional yeast dough but is improved by standing before baking. The result is a crusty loaf with a close texture and good keeping qualities.

100% whole wheat flour 6 cups
Salt 1½ tsp
Water 2 cups

Makes 1 loaf

Combine flour and salt in a mixing bowl and stir in enough warm water to mix to a soft dough. Knead 5 minutes on a lightly floured surface, then return to mixing bowl. Cover with a damp cloth and leave in a warm place overnight or up to 24 hours. Turn out on to a lightly floured surface and knead a further 5 minutes. Place in an oiled 5 x 9 inch loaf pan, cover, and leave in a warm place up to 4 hours. Bake at 400°F about ½ hour, or until easily removed from pan. Cool on a wire rack.

Oatmeal soda bread

This traditional Irish bread does not include yeast and therefore is best served on the day of making.

100% whole wheat flour 4 cups
Oatmeal 1 cup
Cream of tartar 1½ tsp
Baking soda 1 tsp
Salt ½ tsp
Butter or margarine 1 oz
Mixed milk & water, about 2
  cups

Put dry ingredients into a mixing bowl. Rub in butter, then quickly stir in milk and water to give a very soft consistency. Turn mixture into a lightly greased 9″ layer pan and bake at 450°F 15 minutes. Reduce heat to 350°F for a further 15-20 minutes, or until golden. Cool on a wire rack.

Apple & banana bread

A sweet and moist fruit bread that can be sliced and buttered.

Medium-sized apple 1
100% whole wheat flour 4 cups
Dried yeast 1½ tsp
Water ½ cup
Raw sugar ⅓ cup
Salt 1 tsp
Ground cinnamon 1 tsp
Ground nutmeg 1 tsp
Golden seedless raisins ⅓ cup
Small bananas, mashed 2
Lemon, grated rind of ½

Makes 2 loaves

Chop and steam apple until tender. Press through a sieve to make a purée and let cool. Mix together 1 cup flour, yeast, and warm water until smooth, and leave in a warm place until frothy. Combine remaining flour, sugar, salt, spices, and raisins in a bowl. Stir in yeast mixture, apple purée, mashed banana, and lemon and beat well. Divide mixture between two greased 4½ x 8½ inch loaf pans. Let rise in a warm place until mixture reaches top of pans. Bake at 375°F about 35 minutes.

Spiced currant bread

Whole wheat bread dough, using 4 cups flour *(see page 169)*
Molasses 1 tbsp
Organic egg, beaten 1
Currants ⅔ cup
Allspice 2 tsp
Honey to glaze

Makes 1 loaf

Work all ingredients together until well blended. Place dough in a lightly greased 5 x 9 inch loaf pan. Continue as for CRANKS WHOLE WHEAT BREAD *(see page 169)*. Brush top with honey while still warm.

Walnut tea bread

100% whole wheat flour 2½ cups
Oatmeal ½ cup
Wheat germ 2 tbsp
Salt 1 tsp
Walnuts, chopped ½ cup
Dried yeast 1½ tsp
Raw sugar 2 tsp
Water ½-¾ cup
Honey 2 tbsp
Oil 2 tbsp

Makes 1 loaf

In a mixing bowl combine flour, oatmeal, wheat germ, salt, and walnuts. Mix together yeast, sugar, and half the warm water. Leave in a warm place until frothy. Add to mixture with honey, oil, and enough warm water to give a soft dough. Cover and let rise 5 minutes. Knead on a lightly floured surface, then press into a greased 4½ x 8½ inch loaf pan. Cover with oiled plastic wrap and leave in a warm place until mixture reaches top of pan. Remove plastic wrap and bake at 400°F about 30 minutes. Cool on a wire rack. Serve sliced and buttered.

Hot cross buns

These spicy buns are traditionally eaten on Good Friday, but if you leave the crosses off you can make them at any time.

Barley flour 1 cup
100% whole wheat flour 2 cups
Ground cinnamon 2 tsp
Allspice 1½ tsp
Ground nutmeg 1 tsp
Salt 1 tsp
Dried yeast 1½ tsp
Water 4 tbsp
Raw sugar ⅓ cup
Currants ⅔ cup
Milk ½ cup
Butter or margarine, melted
  2 oz
Organic egg, beaten 1
Whole wheat shortcrust pastry
  (see page 181) 2 oz

Glaze
Water 4 tbsp

Makes 12 buns

Put flours, spices and salt into a mixing bowl. Cream yeast with warm water and 1 tsp sugar and leave in a warm place until frothy. Combine flour, yeast mixture, remaining sugar, currants, butter, egg, and enough warm milk to give a soft, manageable dough. Divide mixture into 12 pieces. Knead each one on a lightly floured surface and arrange well apart on floured baking sheets. Leave in a warm place to rise until doubled in size. Roll out pastry and cut into thin strips. Dampen strips and lay 2 on each bun to make a cross. Bake at 375°F about 20 minutes.

Glaze
Heat water and sugar together. Bring to a boil. Brush over buns twice, then let cool.

Jam doughnuts

100% whole wheat flour 2 cups
Salt ½ tsp
Oil 2 tbsp
Dried yeast 1½ tsp
Milk 4 tbsp
Organic egg 1
Jam 10 tsp
Oil for frying
Raw sugar & cinnamon to coat

Makes 10 doughnuts

Put flour, salt, and oil in a bowl. Stir yeast and warm milk together until smooth, then add to flour with egg. Mix to a soft dough. Cover and leave in a warm place to double in size (about ½ hour). Knead lightly, then divide into 10 pieces. Shape each into a round, put 1 tsp jam in the center, and shape dough into a ball. Heat oil and fry doughnuts about 5 minutes, or until golden brown. Drain on paper towels. Sprinkle with sugar mixed with a little cinnamon. Serve warm, if possible.

Chelsea buns

A different way to make fruit buns.

100% whole wheat flour 2½ cups
Dried yeast 1½ tsp
Milk ½ cup
Salt ½ tsp
Margarine 1 oz
Organic egg, beaten 1
Butter or margarine, melted
  2 oz
Mixed dried fruits ¾ cup
Raw sugar ⅓ cup
Honey to glaze

Makes 12 buns

Grease a 11 x 7" cake pan. Put ½ cup flour in a bowl with yeast and warm milk. Beat until smooth. Leave in a warm place until frothy. Meanwhile, put remaining flour and salt in a bowl. Rub in margarine. Add yeast mixture and beaten egg and mix to a soft dough. Knead on a lightly floured surface and then roll out to an oblong 15 x 12". Brush with melted butter and sprinkle with dried fruit and sugar. Starting from a short side, roll up like a jelly roll. Cut into 12 pieces and arrange in the pan cut-side up. Let rise in a warm place, or until buns are touching and have risen to top of pan. Bake at 400°F 20-25 minutes. Brush with warmed honey and let cool in pan.

PASTRY

The basic principles of cooking never change, but obviously recipes and results do, as the ingredients vary–and such is the case with pastry made with 100% whole wheat flour. The texture of shortcrust pastry is coarser than that made with refined white flour, and the absorption qualities of the whole wheat flour may vary a little, so that extra oil or liquid may be necessary to obtain a workable consistency. The flavor and texture of the whole wheat pastry is an altogether different experience to the characterless white product.

There are many people with preconceived ideas about the limitations of 100% whole wheat flour who will be surprised at the good results that can be obtained when it is used to make choux pastry. Success in the making of this pastry depends on the addition of water in the recipe to produce steam during the cooking process.

There are few lovelier sights in the culinary world than a deftly fashioned whole wheat pie shell, with its decorated edge encompassed with absolute harmony in a stoneware dish thrown by a potter.

Whole wheat pastry chart–easy guide to quantities

100% whole wheat flour	Baking powder	Butter and vegetable shortening in equal proportions	Water (approx.)	Made weight of pastry (approx.)
1 cup	1 tsp	2 oz	4 tsp	6 oz
1¼ cups	1½ tsp	2½ oz	2 tbsp	8 oz
1¾ cups	2 tsp	3½ oz	3 tbsp	10 oz
2¼ cups	2½ tsp	4½ oz	3-4 tbsp	14 oz
2½ cups	1 tbsp	5 oz	3-4 tbsp	1 lb
3½ cups	4 tsp	7 oz	4-5 tbsp	1¼ lb

Whole wheat shortcrust pastry

This is the basic recipe to follow for shortcrust pastry when using whole wheat flour.

100% whole wheat flour 1¾ cups
Baking powder 2 tsp
Butter or margarine 1¾ oz
Vegetable shortening ¼ cup
Water 3 tbsp

Makes about 10 oz

Place flour and baking powder in a bowl. Rub in butter and shortening until mixture resembles fine crumbs. Add enough water to give a soft but manageable dough.

VARIATION
Cheese pastry Add 4-6 oz grated Cheddar cheese and ½ tsp mustard powder before water is added.

Hot water crust pastry

This pastry is easy to make and is particularly good for raised savoury pies. It has a firm texture when baked, unlike shortcrust pastry.

100% whole wheat flour 4 cups
Salt 2 tsp
Vegetable shortening ½ cup
Milk or milk & water ½ cup + 3 tbsp

Makes about 1½ lb

Put flour and salt in a bowl. Put vegetable shortening and liquid in a saucepan and heat until shortening is melted. Bring to a boil. Pour on to flour and, with a wooden spoon, mix to form a soft dough. Cover with a damp dish towel or plastic wrap and let rest ½ hour before using.

Choux pastry

Water ½ cup
Butter or margarine 2 oz
100% whole wheat flour 9 tbsp
Organic eggs, beaten 2

Place water and butter in a saucepan. Heat until butter has melted, then bring to a boil. Off heat, stir in flour and beat with a wooden spoon until mixture leaves sides of pan clean and forms a ball. Allow to cool slightly, then beat in egg a little at a time, until thoroughly mixed.

Whole wheat pastry made with oil

An alternative type of shortcrust pastry, which may be a little more difficult to handle.

100% whole wheat flour 2 cups
Baking powder ½ tsp
Salt, pinch
Oil 5 tbsp
Cold water 3 tbsp

Makes about 12 oz

Put flour, baking powder, and salt in a bowl. Whisk oil and water together, then add to dry ingredients. Work together to give a soft, manageable dough. Roll out on a lightly floured surface or between sheets of waxed paper.

PRESERVES & SWEETS

Sugar is the indispensable ingredient in preserves because, quite simply, it is the preservative. Therefore if you are one of those who believe sugar in any form to be harmful to health, you should skip this chapter altogether, or use honey as an alternative (*see Bibliography on page 41*).

As mentioned in the introductory part of this book, we believe refined white sugar to be an unacceptable substance and we use, and recommend for use, only raw sugar that has had the minimum of treatment and retains the naturally occurring minerals and trace elements needed by the body. The molasses form of this sugar is very dark and would produce a very distinctive flavor. Some will like this, but the more generally useful form is the lighter variety that we find very good for all forms of cooking. Of course products made with this will have a different color and flavor, but it is very unlikely that having experienced this quality you will want to return to a white sugar product.

Coarse-cut orange marmalade

A rich, dark and full-flavored marmalade.

Seville oranges 3 lb
Lemon 1
Water 13 cups
Raw sugar 5 lb

Makes about 8 lb

Wash fruit and put it into a preserving pan with water. Cover and simmer gently about 2 hours, or until fruit is soft and skins are easily pierced with a wooden skewer. Remove fruit from pan, and reserve cooking water. Cut fruit in half and remove seeds. Put seeds in a pan with just enough of the reserved water to cover and simmer them while you cut up peel. Slice orange and lemon peel thickly and return it and pulp to preserving pan, with strained liquid from seeds. Bring to a boil. Remove from heat and stir in sugar. Heat very gently, stirring frequently, until sugar dissolves. Bring to a boil, and boil about 20 minutes, or until marmalade jells when tested on a plate. Pour into hot sterilized jars and seal.

Lemon curd

Organic eggs 2
Butter or margarine 4 oz
Lemon, grated rind & juice of 2
Raw sugar 1⅓ cups

Makes 1 lb

Beat eggs and put all ingredients into the top of a double boiler or in a heatproof bowl standing in a pan of simmering water. Stir until sugar has dissolved and continue heating, stirring from time to time, until curd thickens enough to coat the back of a wooden spoon. Pour into hot sterilized jars and seal.

VARIATION
Orange curd Substitute oranges for lemons, and add juice of ½ lemon.

Apple butter

In spite of its misleading name, this preserve is really a thick, firm apple jam.

Cooking apples 3 lb
Water 4 cups
Raw sugar, about 8 cups

Wash and chop apples without peeling or removing cores. Cover with water and simmer gently until pulpy. Sieve and weigh pulp, then return to pan. Add 2⅔ cups sugar for every 1 lb apple pulp. Add

Ground cinnamon (optional)
½ tsp
Ground cloves (optional)
½ tsp

Makes 6 lb

spices, if wished. Heat gently, stirring occasionally until sugar is dissolved, then boil until thick and creamy in consistency. Pour into hot, sterilized jars and seal.

Apple & ginger chutney

This country recipe, which is ideal for using up windfall apples, is given a piquant flavor by the ginger, garlic, and pickling spice.

Cider vinegar 3 cups
Raw sugar 4 cups
Pickling spice 1 tbsp
Cooking apples 2¼ lb
Medium-sized onions 2
Fresh ginger ¼ lb
Garlic cloves 2 large
Salt 2 tsp
Golden seedless raisins ⅔ cup

Makes about 4 lb

Heat vinegar and sugar slowly in a large saucepan until sugar is dissolved. Meanwhile, tie pickling spice in a small piece of cheesecloth. Core and chop apples, skin and chop onion, peel and grate ginger, and peel and crush garlic. Add all ingredients to pan, bring to a boil, reduce heat, and simmer, stirring occasionally, about 2 hours, or until mixture is thick and no excess liquid remains. Remove pickling spice. Pour chutney into hot, sterilized jars and seal.

Fruit & nut chews

These sweets are quick and easy to make as there is no sugar-boiling involved.

Raisins ⅔ cup
Pitted dates ¾ cup
Walnuts ¾ cup
Dried coconut ⅔ cup

Makes about 24

Using a food processor fitted with a coarse blade, mince raisins, dates, and walnuts together. Add coconut and work mixture with fingertips until it binds. Form into thin rolls and cut into bite-sized pieces.

Marzipan shapes

Marzipan (see page 139) 1 cup
Walnut halves
Dates 12

Makes 24

Walnut Rounds
Roll half the marzipan into 12 balls. Press a walnut half on to each.

Date Barrels
Remove pits from dates. Shape remaining marzipan into 12 "barrel" shapes and press into middle of each date.

Coconut bars

This whole food adaptation of coconut bars will keep in the refrigerator for about one week.

Cream cheese ½ cup
Raw sugar ⅓ cup
Dried coconut 1⅓ cups
Mixed nuts, finely ground ½ cup

Makes about 20 bars

Work all ingredients together until evenly mixed. Shape into a bar, then cut into pieces. Leave on waxed paper to dry.

Carob fudge

A soft-textured sweet, rather like fudge.

Butter or margarine 4 tbsp
Carob powder ¼ cup
Honey 2 tbsp
Soy flour ¼ cup
Ground almonds ⅔ cup
Vanilla extract 1 tsp
Almonds, ground or finely chopped 3 tbsp

Cream butter and carob powder until well mixed. Add the next 4 ingredients and mix thoroughly. Sprinkle ground almonds on a clean, dry working surface and shape the fudge into a roll, coating with almonds. Cut into bite-sized pieces. Keep in refrigerator until needed.

VARIATION
Sesame fudge Replace 3 tbsp ground almonds with 3 tbsp toasted sesame seeds.

Dried apricot & almond jam

A delicious whole-fruit jam that can be made at any time of the year. The whole almonds may be omitted if wished.

Dried apricots 1 lb
Lemon, juice of 1
Raw sugar 8 cups
Whole almonds, blanched ⅔ cup

Makes about 5 lb

Wash apricots, then cover with 6 cups water and let soak 24 hours. Put fruit with water and lemon juice in a large saucepan or preserving pan and simmer ½ hour. Add sugar, and almonds if wished, and stir over low heat until sugar is dissolved. Bring to a boil and boil rapidly, stirring frequently, until jam jells when tested on a plate. Pour into hot sterilized jars and seal. Cool and store.

DRINKS

One tends to overlook the fact that a drink is often more than just liquid and can really be a liquid food, and as such can be at least as nourishing as solid food. In fact it is possible to get a considerably bigger intake of vitamins and minerals from raw fruit and vegetables by drinking the extracted juices than by trying to munch through them in their solid state. But is is important to remember to drink these juices slowly (preferably through a straw) because of the concentration of the food and the time needed to digest it.

In the Bircher-Benner Sanatorium in Zurich, Switzerland, they specialize in the treatment of degenerative diseases with the use of raw foods and juices and achieve many wonderful results, even with cases labeled incurable by the medical profession. They say that raw juices are the "Life Blood" of the vegetables, containing the vital enzymes and digestive factors so important for keeping our bodies in a healthy condition.

We introduced raw juices on our menu from the time we first opened Cranks in 1961, producing them laboriously in domestic juice extractors, and even to this day with a vastly bigger business we still have to use these small-scale juicers. A juice extractor should not be confused with a blender. The extractor operates by forcing vegetables or hard fruit down on to a very high revolution grater plate that has the effect of throwing the juices to the outer circumference by centrifugal force through a sieve and then out of the machine through a spout. The residual roughage is either collected and occasionally emptied or is ejected during the operation. A blender, on the other hand, is a goblet at the bottom of which are fast rotating and cutting blades. Chopped fruit or vegetables are dropped into a liquid (water, stock, or juice) and are chopped up very finely by the blades and blended evenly with the liquid until they have a smooth creamy consistency.

The flavor of the extracted juices defies description–they seem to radiate a pure life force that puts them on another plane from other foods. Many other healthy and flavorsome drinks, of course, such as yeast-based drinks, herb teas, and others, are good alternatives to coffee, chocolate, and malted drinks, which are often harmful to health. The following chart should assist those starting out on the adventure of changing to a health food regime.

Some drinks that are commonly consumed can be harmful to health when drunk on a regular basis. Tea and coffee are stimulants and can be damaging to the nervous and digestive systems. We have set out below some alternatives as a guide for those wishing to change to a more healthy intake.

INSTEAD OF	DRINK
Fresh or instant coffee	Dandelion coffee Decaffeinated coffee Cereal grain coffee

Tea	Maté tea, possibly with just a
	    pinch of your favorite
	    black tea
	Fresh herb or tisane teas

Wine	Apple juice (organic) Grape juice *Ideal for drinking and driving*

Tap water (mostly recycled many
    times, and often fluorinated)
	Bottled mineral water, e.g.,
	    Vichy, Perrier

Bottled soft drinks	Natural fruit juices
	    diluted with sparkling
	    mineral water

Bovril	Vegex
Cocoa and drinking chocolate	Carob drink

Freshly extracted vegetable & fruit juices

Freshly extracted juices have always been a specialty in Cranks since its opening in 1961, and Cranks is often asked "How do we make them at home, does it take long, is it worth the trouble?" The answer to the last question is definitely "Yes." The reward of exciting flavors and absolutely "instant vitamins" ensures that all the drinks are worth the trouble. Whether they are served on their own or mixed with other ingredients, there is a wide range of flavors.

Although juicing is a fairly time-consuming process, the preparation of the raw ingredients is simple, and with the help of an electric juice separator you can have freshly extracted juices without much effort.

Extracted juices are very concentrated and should be taken in moderation–Gaylord Hauser recommends 2 cups of juice a day! To give you an idea of amounts of raw materials required:

1 lb carrots produces ⅔ cup juice
1 lb apples produces ⅔ cup juice
1 lb tomatoes produces 1 cup juice
1 lb blackberries produces 1 cup juice

There are many excellent books on the subject of juicing, and these are referred to in the Bibliography *(see page 41)*.

Preparation for extracted juices

Watercress juice. A dark green juice, best used in combination with other juices. Wash watercress leaves and stalks in a colander. Feed through the extractor in small bunches, adding a little water to aid extraction.

Spinach juice. A dark green juice, very concentrated and best used with other juices or mixed with yogurt and a pinch of sea salt. Wash leaves and stalks well and feed small handfuls through the extractor with a little water.

Parsley & mint juice. Another dark green juice that should be combined with carrot or tomato–the method is as for spinach.

Cabbage juice. Strongly flavored but good combined with other juices. It is best to use young green cabbage. Wash well and coarsely chop. Feed through extractor with a little water.

Carrot juice. This juice has a wonderful flavor and color and mixes well with other juices. Wash carrots well but do not peel or top and tail. Cut into convenient chunks to fit extractor. Add a little lemon juice after juicing as this helps to keep its color and prevents it going brown.

Celery juice. This juice is best used mixed with another juice as it is quite strong. Add a little lemon juice to prevent discoloration and store away from bright light. Wash celery, including leaves, and cut into convenient lengths.

Cucumber juice. In spite of a bland flavor, one cucumber will yield a lot of juice compared with other vegetables. Wash cucumber and cut up. It is delicious blended with a little lemon juice and honey.

Apple juice. This makes a very tasty drink and combines well with most of the vegetable juices. Always add lemon juice to prevent discoloration. Wash and cup up apples but do not peel or core. Remove any imperfections.

Tomato juice. A lovely drink that tastes so different from canned tomato juice. Wash and chop tomatoes. It combines well with yogurt, and a pinch of sea salt improves the flavor.

Pineapple juice. Peel and cut up into convenient pieces to fit the extractor. Makes a delicious juice for drinks and fruit-salad syrup.

Grape juice. A tasty drink and a juice that combines well with other juices. Wash grapes and feed through extractor. It also makes a good base for fruit salads.

Soft fruit juices. Pick over fruits and push through a sieve or feed through juice extractor. It is sometimes necessary to pour a little water through at the same time.

Keep all extracted juices in the refrigerator and cover.

Recipes for drinks as served in Cranks

Carrot, apple (or orange) & honey. Measure 1 part apple (or orange) juice and 4 parts carrot juice into a blender. Add honey to taste and blend a few seconds.

Mixed vegetable. Measure 2 parts carrot juice and 1 part each of celery and cucumber juice into a blender. Blend a few seconds.

Carrot & spinach (or watercress). Measure 3 parts carrot juice and 1 part spinach (or watercress) juice into a blender. Blend a few seconds.

Apple & cabbage. Measure 3 parts apple juice and 1 part cabbage juice into a blender. Blend a few seconds.

Cucumber, lemon & honey. Measure 3 parts cucumber juice and 1 part lemon juice into a blender. Add honey to sweeten and blend a few seconds.

Watercress, tomato & apple. Measure 1 part each of watercress juice and tomato juice and 2 parts apple juice into a blender. Blend a few seconds.

Lemon (or orange) fizz. Wash and chop ½ lemon (or orange) and place in a blender. Pour on sufficient water to cover and blend until smooth. Strain through a fine nylon sieve into a glass, or jug, and top with Perrier water. Sweeten to taste with honey, if wished.

Yogurt, milk & honey drink. Put ½ cup each fresh milk and natural yogurt in a blender. Add 1-2 tsp honey and blend until smooth. Serve chilled.

Juice, yogurt & milk drink. The juice may be freshly extracted or the bottled kind. Use any flavor you like. Salt can be added to savoury drinks. A little honey or raw sugar can be added to sweet drinks. Put ½ cup fruit or vegetable juice and ⅓ cup each fresh milk and natural yogurt in a blender. Blend until smooth. Serve chilled.

Tiger's milk. This is a Gaylord Hauser recipe. Put ½ cup each fresh milk and orange juice in a blender. Add 2 tsp skim milk powder and 1 tsp each Brewers' yeast and molasses. Blend until smooth and serve chilled.

Banana milk. Put a peeled ripe banana and 1 cup fresh milk in a blender. Blend until smooth. Serve chilled.

Curvacious cocktail. This is a Gaylord Hauser recipe. Put ⅔ cup fresh orange juice, 1 organic egg, 1 tbsp wheat germ, and 1 tsp honey in a blender. Blend until smooth and serve chilled.

Yogurt, milk & fruit drink. Put ⅔ cup fresh fruit (raspberries, strawberries, pitted apricots, etc.), ½ cup natural yogurt, and 1 cup milk into a blender. Add raw sugar or honey to taste and blend until smooth. Strain, if wished, before serving.

Cranks homemade lemonade

This lovely drink is made every day in Cranks using fresh lemons and raw sugar. Occasionally when the sugar is extra dark it is nick-named "Thames Mud" and some of our foreign customers wonder what on earth it is! The sharp, fresh flavor bears absolutely no relationship to the present-day bottled variety found in the supermarket–how could a simple drink like this have deteriorated so much?

It is definitely well worth the effort to buy extra lemons and make this at home. The recipe suggests raw sugar, but it is quite possible to use honey instead, and some people, particularly children, might prefer this. The strength of lemons varies considerably and it may be advisable to dilute the lemonade, particularly for children who may not have experienced the flavor of real lemons and could be put off if it is served too strong.

Lemons 4
Raw brown sugar 1 cup
Boiling water 3¾ cups

Makes about 3¾ cups

Scrub lemons, halve, then squeeze out juice. Place juice and pulp in a large jug or bowl with sugar and pour 1¼ cups boiling water over. Stir until sugar dissolves. Add lemon halves and another 2½ cups boiling water. Stir well, then cover and let cool. Strain, squeezing out juice from lemon halves and serve.

Lemon brose

This is a real old-fashioned drink, based on oatmeal, that is easy to make, nutritious and satisfying–and is especially suitable for children.

Oatmeal ½ cup
Raw sugar 1 tbsp
Lemon 1
Water 1 cup

Makes ⅔ cup

Put oatmeal in a jug with raw sugar. Squeeze juice from lemon and add to oatmeal together with lemon halves. Pour 1 cup boiling water over and stir well. Cover and let cool. Strain, squeezing out juice from lemon halves, thin to desired consistency with water, and serve.

VARIATION
Orange Brose Substitute 1 orange for 1 lemon.

If wished, this drink may be served warm. A shot of whisky gives a "kick!" The same recipe can be used for Lemon or Orange Barley Drink–use barley flakes instead of oatmeal.

Herb tea or tisane

Many people grow herbs in their garden and use them for cooking, but few use them for making drinks. Herb teas are considered to be beneficial to the body, each herb having specific qualities.

For fresh herb teas, pick a large sprig of mint, lemon balm, or other fresh herb, wash carefully, then place in a small jug, and pour on boiling water. Leave to infuse for up to 5 minutes, then strain into a cup. It is sometimes possible to buy a glass teapot for making herb teas–with this you can see the infusion as well as taste it.

There is, of course, a great variety of herb teabags sold in health food stores–rosehip, camomile, lime flower, peppermint, and many others–and these, apart from being very convenient to use, make a most acceptable substitute for coffee or tea. Simply place one tea bag in a cup or small jug, and pour on boiling water. Leave for a few minutes, remove tea bag and then drink–sweeten with a little honey if desired.

Hot drinks

Carob milk. Mix 2-3 tsp carob powder with a little cold milk measured from 1 cup until there is a smooth paste. Heat remaining milk and pour over carob paste, stirring. Sweeten if wished. This drink can also be served chilled.

Honey & lemon. Put 1 tsp honey, 1 tbsp lemon juice, and a slice of lemon in a glass. Place a metal spoon in the glass then pour in ½ cup boiling water. Stir and serve. If wished, a shot of whisky or rum can be added.

VARIATION
Use a small orange instead of lemon.

Dandelion root "coffee." For each cup: Put 1 tsp dandelion root in a saucepan with ⅔ cup water. Bring to a boil, reduce heat, and simmer 10 minutes. Strain, and serve as coffee, with or without milk.

Honegar. Put 1 tsp each cider vinegar and honey into a glass. Place a metal spoon in the glass and stir in ½ cup hot water until honey dissolves.

Clear mineral broth–makes about 3¾ cups. Prepare and coarsely chop a celery heart, one large onion, ½ cup spinach, 2 sticks celery, and 2 medium-sized carrots. Place in a saucepan with 3¾ cups water, 1 tsp salt, and a few parsley sprigs. Cover and simmer about 30 minutes, then strain. Serve at once. The broth may be covered and refrigerated and reheated as required.

Index

For general cookery information, see under *Culinary know-how.*